LITTLE
MICHAEL HORROR

LARRY MONROE

tate publishing
CHILDREN'S DIVISION

Little Michael Horror
Copyright © 2016 by Larry Monroe. All rights reserved.

This title is also available as a Tate Out Loud product. Visit www.tatepublishing.com for more information.

No part of this publication may be reproduced, stored in a retrieval system or transmitted in any way by any means, electronic, mechanical, photocopy, recording or otherwise without the prior permission of the author except as provided by USA copyright law.

The opinions expressed by the author are not necessarily those of Tate Publishing, LLC.

This novel is a work of fiction. Names, descriptions, entities, and incidents included in the story are products of the author's imagination. Any resemblance to actual persons, events, and entities is entirely coincidental.

Published by Tate Publishing & Enterprises, LLC
127 E. Trade Center Terrace | Mustang, Oklahoma 73064 USA
1.888.361.9473 | www.tatepublishing.com

Tate Publishing is committed to excellence in the publishing industry. The company reflects the philosophy established by the founders, based on Psalm 68:11,
"The Lord gave the word and great was the company of those who published it."

Book design copyright © 2016 by Tate Publishing, LLC. All rights reserved.
Cover and interior design by Ralph Lim

Published in the United States of America

ISBN: 978-1-68207-002-4
1. Fiction / Fantasy / Paranormal
2. Fiction / Religious
16.05.17

THE MODERN DAY Prince of Horror tales! I take the UN-real and make it seem real; one cannot say when they enter into my world of Horror, they will leave the same way they entered. I believe that everyone has a Horror tale to tell in this; also this world is based on Horror tales. This is a story about a little boy name Michael who was born evil, plus his soul was possessed. This chilling tale will also make you think twice about the things you believe in and what you say that you don't believe in. This is a strange story about a young couple (Mitchell and Ebony) who decided to turn their backs on their religious belief and live their own lives for once. This story deals with spiritual forces that end up possessing a little child that the Robinson's had out of wedlock. The child was born with a very strange behavior problem and the family became dysfunctional with each other trying to understand their child. As the child got older his evilness grew darker and darker, his parents begin to get frighten of him and decided to seek help for there son. Michael later developed a trust for blood and wicket acts towards people, Later the parents find out that a strange man in red had mad a deal for Little Michael's soul. The mother of Little Michael later decides to battle the dark angel for her son's soul, and the father hunts down the person responsible for their pain. A turn comes about when darker forces intervene and the parent goes on a witch hunt together. This story may send chills up your spin but believe me its good reading so sit back then take a deep breath and begin. Problems plus he began sheltering

.....

December 5th, 1951 on the lower east side of Manhattan, around the Ave D section, a young man name (Mitchell Robinson) and his girl friend (Ebony walker) stayed in an old tenement building in the middle of the block. Ebony was nine mouths pregnant and was ready to give birth that night, Mitchell rushed his girl friend to the Hospital so that she can give birth to their little baby boy. Mitchell stood there in the waiting room waiting for Ebony's parent's to get to the Hospital but only the mother arrived. The Doctor came out and asked the mother to come see her daughter and Mitchell decided to stay in the waiting room for the moment. As Mitchell sat down in the chair he began to think back when Ebony and he first met, Mitchell became drossy and began to think back. The two met in Ebony's Fathers Church in the upper east side of Manhattan, It was a small Pentecostal Church and the people were all close to each other. Mitchell's Father was the head Deacon of the Church and his mother was the Deaconess. Ebony's father was the Bishop and her mother was the first lady, Mitchell was the junior deacon of the Church and Ebony just sung in the Church choir. Mitchell is a very positive and bright young man; who always dreamed of being his own boss. He also dreamed about having a family of his own one day, plus one day being about the better serves his community. Mitchell is a good student and also he was a very good cartoonist for a child his age, his imagination was out standing and he could create stories like never before. Any thing that he Pictured in his head he could draw it, Mitchell often found himself drawing pictures of Ebony singing in front of the church. Mitchell looked a lot like his father but he looked at life much different then his father, the father pretty much accepted what was placed in front of him, but Mitchell did not. He was the strong silent type, but he went after things that he wanted. Now Ebony was the sweet gentle educated type who taught a lot, and paid very close attention to things around her. Ebony is also a good student that always bought home good grades and always listened to her parents, she had dreams of one day owning her own day care center and one day going to Africa to teach. Mitchell was nineteen at the time and Ebony was eighteen years old and they always stared at each other from across the room of the Church. They always noticed each other but never had the nerve to say anything; they just smile and gazed into each others eyes from across the room. On Mitchell's twentieth birthday he finally got the nerve to ask Ebony out on a date, he took her to a nice soul food restaurant in Harlem! The Restaurant was run by a Minister called Brother Devine, who was a well known person in the neighborhood,

Mitchell and Ebony were still in their Sunday best! The two looked fantastic together, Mitchell spend his whole pay check on Ebony; Mitchell worked at a bakery store on 125th street (Goods Bakery). Ebony baby sat after school plus she help totter students, at dinner Mitchell told Ebony that one day he was going to be the owner of his own business. He also told her that he would be well known in the community; Ebony just smiled at him and told him that anything is possible with God and she believed in him. Their dinner came and the waiter brought then two rib dinners specials with two tall glasses of iced tea, the smell was delicious. As the two sat down and dined, Mitchell gazed into Ebony's eyes and smiled; he then reached into his pocket and pulled out neck lace and gave it to her. Ebony and looked at Mitchell with love in her eyes, she then reached over and accepted the gift and told him that it was beautiful. Mitchell bent over the table and told her that he hopes that she ends up being his wife. Ebony looked at him and said" How do you know I would be a good wife for you? Mitchell looked her in the eyes and told her that his heart told him so and his heart doesn't lie. Then Ebony reached over and gave him a kiss and they went back to eating their dinner, right after dinner Mitchell took her to the movies to see Godzilla vs. King Kong. After the Movie they took a walk in the park and then he took her home, he then gave her a kiss and then went back home. Mouths passed and Mitchell and Ebony drew closer and closer, they been on several dates and winded up falling in love, the two continued to see each other until they ended up getting involved with each other. For a while they kept it a secret but later they decided to tell their parents, and at that time Mitchell wanted to get his own place. Later Mitchell told his mother and father that he was seeing the Bishop's daughter and his parents were pleased to hear that. A few days later Ebony told her parents the news but the father was not pleased to here that, he was dead set against it. The mother was happy for them but the father continued to tell Ebony that the lord did not pick him for her. Ebony looked at her father and told him that she love Mitchell and she is grown now so she really don't need his approval. Then she went to her room and slammed the door, Ebony's mother looked at the Bishop and told him that she is an adult now and she will make the right choice. Then she stood up and told him that Mitchell is a nice and decent boy who knows what he wants, and then she went into Ebony's room to talk to her and ask her to forgive him. Then she asked Ebony to excuse her father's ignorance and maybe she should give him some time to come to his senses. She looked at her mother then she hugged her with tears in her eyes, uttering that she really love Mitchell. Ebony's mother then told her that her father did not want her with her father but she still married him. Ebony looked at her and said for real mom! And the mother smiled and said it's true, my father felt that he was a loser. Ebony wiped her eyes and told her mother that Mitchell wants to marry her; Ms Walker smiled and told her that she should pray on it and God would help you make the right decision. Ebony gave her mother a kiss and told her that she was going to call Mitchell with the good news, and then Ms Walker got off the bed and went back into the living room. Mr. and Mrs. Walker were in the living discussing the matter of their daughter being with Mitchell Robinson. The father believed that Mitchell was not good enough for his little girl and that didn't want it either, Mrs. Walker looked at him and told that God never said that and he knows it. Mr. Walker became upset and walked out the living room and went into the bedroom to pray and his wife went into the kitchen to fix dinner. Days began to past and Ebony confined in Mitchell for support and he was more then happy to do so, Mitchell told Ebony that he was looking for another job so he can take care of her. Later in the week Mitchell found an extra job at a junk yard on Hunts point, he also found an apartment in the lower east side of Manhattan. Ebony and her father was going at it for weeks about her dating Mitchell and she finally told her father and mother that she was leaving home for good. The mother tried to talk her out of it but her father told her to get out and he would let the Lord deal with her. Ebony became heated and left the house, and then as she made her way to the side walk she heard her mother yelling at her father. She heard her telling him that he was wrong and she has the right to like who ever she wants to, but the Father still stood his grounds about the matter. Ebony then walked to a nearby pay phone and called Mitchell and told him what just happen then he told her to come live with him. She told him that she was going to stay at a friend's house in the Bronx, and then he told her that if she changes her mine; his door is always open. She then told him that she had to call him back because she had to call her friend (Brenda) to see if it was ok for her to come over now. She then hung up the phone and called Brenda but she couldn't let her stay because she did not have enough room. Ebony began to feel that she did not have anyone on her side so she began calling her family members but they all was siding with her father. At first Ebony was against moving in with her boy friend without them being married but she realized that she had to do what she felt was best for her and not her father. So she called back Mitchell and asked him to come pick her up so he called some friends and they went to get Ebony's things from her room while the Bishop was at service. They moved her to Mitchell's apartment and he promised her that he will always keep her happy, Ebony told him that she believed in him and that she knows everything will be fine between them. The dream moved on to when they got older and they began shaping into good strong respectful people, Mitchell grew into a smooth talking laid back brother and Ebony became a sweet soft spoken woman who trusted in the lord. Ebony had graduated and she went to find her a job, she ended up working at a few Hotels sites as a chamber maid. Mitchell on the other hand was loading and unloading trucks on his spare time, the two were doing well for the moment. Ebony worked at the Hotels for two years until she landed with a coffee factory job from a local temp agency, The Coffee Factory Company was located on Baltic Ave in lower Brooklyn. The two began to furnish their apartment better and began inviting friends and neighbors over and they realize that it was right to move together. Mitchell and Ebony came from good hard working family, who raised them with strong working values and they both was determent to make it on their own. They shared a one bed room apartment and were just getting bye but the two of them kept the bills paid and food on their table. Mitchell worked very hard and Ebony did plus she was very good in saving money, that is why their bank account grew bigger and bigger. Mitchell would work two to three jobs to bring home money for his women and Ebony would bring home toys so that she can sell them for extra cash. The Holidays came and Mitchell took Ebony to his parent's house for dinner and while they were dinning Mitchell found out that his father had back slid. He left the Church and ended up becoming the leader of a strange religious cult, his mother then told him that she had tried to talk him out of it but he denounced God and then left her. She then told him that the cult was called Children of the First Order (C.O.T.F.O.) then she said he had disappeared and couldn't be found. Mitchell looked at his mother and asked her was it because he decided to be with Ebony that he started to lose his mine? The mother said no and that he really liked Ebony and want you're to be together, and then told him that his father was proud of his choice to leave God. Then she told him that he was complaining about the way Church people acted towards each other plus the way the Bishop started acting towards him after you too moved together. Mitchell 's mother told him to ask God to forgive him because she did, then she told him that the last thing he said before he left was that he wants to live some where in the Peekskill mountains. Mitchell became very upset that his father would do something like that to his Family, and then he told his mother that he would always be there for her. They all sat down to dinner and later that evening Ebony began feeling sick so Mitchell took her back home so she can get some rest. Around 1:30 a.m. Ebony got out of the bed and went the bathroom to varmint, Mitchell heard her and got out of his bed and went to see what was wrong with her!" what's wrong Honey? Mitchell yelled out! After that Mitchell helped Ebony to get and he did also. Mitchell then called a cab and took her to the Hospital and they later found out that she was five mouths pregnant. Mitchell stood there in a daze until the Doctor came and told him that his girl was calling for him. The dream began to fade and he slowly came back to his senses then he went to see Ebony. Ebony lay in her bed feeling weak and drained plus her confidence level was very low, she began to complain that God was not pleased with them. Mitchell looked at her and told her that God doesn't have the problem with us, it's my Father! God has a problem with. Ebony's mother went to hug her and she began feeling cold, then she grabbed her mother and began crying asking God to forgive her. Her mother began to tear also telling Ebony that God was not dis- pleased with them and she need to relax so that the baby would come out healthy. Mitchell became upset and told Ebony that her father was still controlling their lives and he was sick of it, Ebony's mother told Mitchell to relax and watch his tone with her baby. Mitchell told Ebony and her mother that he was sorry but her father is a wacked out religious nut who took things to far. Also that he was sick and tired of her father's bull about God! Mitchell then looked at his wife and said that God probably didn't know who they were; or better yet didn't care what they did with each other. Ebony covered her face and began to burst into tears and her mother looked at Mitchell and told him that she was surprised at him, then she told him that God helps bring joy and that it was God that brought the two of you together. Mitchell looked at Ebony and seen her in tears so he began feeling bad about what he just said so he went over to her and gave her a hug and kiss. He then told her that he loves her and that they would be ok no matter what anyone says; Ebony told Mitchell that she was scared. Her mother told her that God want them together and don't worry, Later that night when Ebony was in the bed sleeping she began to feel a shape pain so she jumped up and began screaming! Mitchell then woke up and ran over to her and held her tight! He then looked at her and seen that she was looking kind of pale so he rang for the Doctor. Then one of the nurses came in and saw that Ebony was dehydrated and looking very weak, then she began to grow weaker by the moment and Mitchell noticed it and asked the nurse what was wrong with his women. The Doctor came and they checked her and found out that the baby was lacking in nutrients and he was draining her of hers. The child was in need food that was pasted down from mother to child in it growing stages, Even though Ebony was eating healthy the child was not receiving it for some reason. Mitchell began to worry rather Ebony was right about God not being pleased with what they have done. Ebony told the doctor that she always ate right and she can't understand why this is happening to her then the doctor gave her a few treatments and she began feeling and looking better. She then turned to Mitchell and told him that they needed to go back to Church and ask the Lord to forgive them for their sins. Mitchell then looked at her and told her that if she wanted to go back to Church it was ok with him. Then he gave her a kiss. He then told her that he would never stray away from the Lords house ever again but in his heart he felted that Ebony's father just filled her head up with bull. In Mitchell's mind Ebony's father was a sick phony conman who used Gods word to keep people as a prisoner in his Church. He told Ebony what she wanted to hear so that she would stay calm for the babies well being but in his heart he knew that he was right about her Father. Then he turned to the Doctor then asked" was Ebony and his child going to be alright! Then the doctor checked her and told Mitchell that she was about to give birth soon and that he felted it would be best that they get some rest now. Mitchell looked at Ebony and told the doctor to call him if he needed him and he would be right back. Then Mitchell grabbed his coat and left the Hospital with Ebony's mother they caught a cab and Mitchell dropped her off at her home. Mitchell then told the cab driver to take him home down in lower Manhattan, When he got into the house he called his boss, then he told him that his lady was about to give birth and that he needed some time off. His boss told him to take his sick days, that way he can still get paid and he would see him when he get back. Mitchell hung up the phone then began to fix him some food when he began feeling strange! Like someone was watching him, Mitchell turned towards the entrance of the kitchen but he did not see any one there so he just ignored it and continued cooking. But when he sat down at the table he began feeling funny again, like someone was watching him again and the place was feel strange to him. Mitchell then rest his hands a pond his head and in back of him was a strange glowing figure that appeared on the back wall. Mitchell turned slowly toward it and saw an old disfigured man staring at him, Mitchell looked at him and yelled out" Demon be gone! Then he got up and grabbed a knife and came toward it. The strange old man began to vibrate and then he disappeared, Mitchell dropped the knife and began to get nerviest. Then Mitchell began hearing a voice telling him that he was not going to harm him! And Mitchell began yelling in fear for him to leave him alone. Then the voice told him that his father had made a pack with the Devil and Mitchell looked around and asked the voice what he was talking about! And the strange figure reappeared! Mitchell then turned off his food and walked over to the strange old man. The old man looked at Mitchell and told him that the Devil needed a child to rule on earth and that his father promised his first grandson. Mitchell stood there confused then he told the strange old man that he did not believe his father was capable of that. The strange old man looked at him and told him that he was warned and that he would never come again. Then the strange old man stood up and disappeared and Mitchell walked back to the chair in the kitchen and sat down. Mitchell got up and went to the stove to fix his plate and then he sat back down at the table and began eating. As he sat there eating began thinking about what the strange old man told him, he then sat up and looked up and began to ask God was he loosing his mind. Then he froze for a moment and then he asked God did he send that man to warn that his father was really a Devil worshiper. He did not get an answer so he went back to eating his food, then after ward he went to take a shower and relax. Later that afternoon Mitchell woke up then got dressed and went to the living room to watch television. Around 2:30 p.m. Mitchell received a call from the Hospital informing him that Ebony's water had broke and that she was going into the delivery room. Mitchell then put on his jacket and rushed to the Hospital to be by a side but he was kind of scared to see her give birth. The Doctor then asked him did he want to be in the delivery room with her but he told him that he was ok. Mitchell then began pacing around for hours mumbling to him self about God being un-fair to them for leaving that no good Church. Then he finally sat down to get his nerves in order and ended up falling asleep and shortly he was awakened by a strange light. When he opened his eyes he saw his Father badly disfigured with chunks of flesh hanging off of his face. Mitchell stood there in shock as his father spoke to him" Your child is to be the next on the thorn in Hell! Mitchell's father uttered! Mitchell nervously replied" What the heck are you talking about! Then Mitchell tried to get up and attack his father but he could not move a muscle. Mitchell then began yelling and calling his father a sick and crazy loser, his father then began laughing as he disappeared. He then began screaming out his fathers name as he was awakened by the Doctor, telling him that he was the proud father of a seven pound baby boy. Mitchell then jumped up and ran into the room where Ebony was and gave her a big kiss; she looked at him and told him that she wanted to name him Michael after his father. Mitchell's middle name was Michael but he never used it because he did not care for his father much. Mitchell did not want to argue with her about the name so he went along with it but he felt that his father was crazy and always hated him as a child. Ebony seemed to love the name so Mitchell agreed to it so that he could please her in any way. Little Michael was a handsome little thing with soft curly hair and light brown eyes, he was so handsome and it was a proud day for the couple. Mitchell then smiled and told Ebony that God blessed them with a strong Nubian king and it was time to stand proud. The day was so over whelming to him that he totally forgot what his father's ghost has said to him about his new born son. That night Mitchell went home feeling good about being a father so he went to the neighborhood liquor store and brought him self a bottle rum to celebrate. Mitchell went up stares and rolled up a joint from his secret stash and lit it up, and then he sat in the living room and turn on the television. He then sat back and began to relax for the moment when he got a phone call from one of his friends; Mitchell began telling his friend that this was the greatest time of his life. Later in the week Mitchell ended up bring Ebony and his son home; he had decorated their room up to welcome the newest member to their family. The room was full of brand new baby things, Ebony took a leave from work to raise their little son while Mitchell took other side to make ends meat to feed his family. Things was hard but they still stayed strong, it was very difficult for blacks with children back then and the jobs was hard to find especially without a degree of any kind. Mitchell was a very determined man who knew what he wanted and he was not going to let anyone stop him from getting what he wanted. Ebony was a well like person who tried to live as best as she could to the teaching of the Church and thy made a lovely couple. Mitchell did a lot of off the books work and he was never home much but Ebony understood because she knew it was for the family. So she stood home and raised Little Michael the best way she could, Ebony's mother dropped by to help out time from time. The apartment was very well kept and Mitchell brought home the money, Little Michael was a child that needed a lot of attention because of his strange behavior. Ebony began to notice that Little Michael never cried or smiled at any time, he just looked at her with a blank look on his face. Little Michael never blinked his eyes or ever said a word; he just crawled around the house looking at the walls. As Little Michael grew older he began to get stranger and stranger in his behavior, Little Michael became scarier to his mothers family and friends. Ebony was visited by her aunt and uncle and when they saw the way little Michael was behaving they told her that he was possessed by the Devil. Little Michael always crawled around with his head down and never showed any emotion to anyone. Ebony always kept a picture of Jesus on her wall and Little Michael always looked at it with a blank look. As Ebony's aunt and uncle sat at the table talking about Little Michael he crawled by them and stopped and stared at them like he knew that they were talking bad about him. The aunt turn and saw Little Michael looking at then and told Ebony that she thinks he knows that he is the center of the conversation. Ebony looked at them then said that he was only a baby and that is ridiculous and they went back to talking, Little Michael's then stood up and walked to the back room. The uncle glanced and saw Little Michael walk away and he yelled for the other to look but he was gone. They ran to the door way and did not see Little Michael on the floor crawling so they went to the back room and found him on the floor looking at the walls. The uncle looked at Ebony, then told her that he seen Little Michael get off the floor and walk away, she looked at him like he was crazy and walked back to the kitchen. The uncle looked at him and Little Michael turned his head and smiled! Then the uncle became scared and walked back to the kitchen with a fearful look on his face. Ebony was in the Kitchen telling her aunt that she felted that her son was a little slow and not possessed and she wishes that she would stop saying that! The aunt told her that her father had told the Church that because you back slid from God that you and your child is Dammed! Ebony became angry and asked her to leave her house and never come back. The aunt and uncle got up and walked towards the door and saw Little Michael standing in the door way of his mother room with his eyes glowing. They became scared and ran out the door screaming in fear, Ebony came out and ran to the front door to see what happen but they had already ran down the stairs. Ebony then turned around and saw Little Michael sitting on the floor clapping his hands, so she went over to him and picked him up and gave him a kiss. As the aunt and uncle left the building and walked down the street to go to the bus stop something fell out of the ski and cut them in half at the Connor of the side walk. That night Mitchell came home and saw that someone had got killed on his block but he did not pay it any attention. He went to his building and went upstairs to his family; he got in the house and found Ebony on the phone. Mitchell then looked at his wife and told her that they live in a messed up neighborhood. Mitchell then went over to his women and gave her a kiss, and then he asked her how her day was! Ebony then looked at him and told him that her aunt and uncle was just killed leaving their home, Mitchell looked at her and said" that was them? Oh my God! Then he went to the window and told Ebony to look but she did not want to! Little Michael was sitting in the Living room looking at the walls clapping his hand. Mitchell saw Little Michael and went over to him and picked him up and gave him a kiss and put him back down and watched him crawl away. Then he sat down in the living room and watch television until dinner was ready, Mitchell then told Ebony that he was going to get a better job so that he could move them out of this rat infested hole in the wall. Then he began uttering about how the building was drug infested and that a one bed room was not good enough for his family. Then he said that he was tire of seeing bums laying in the hallway and hooker having sex on the stair cases also he was sick of it, and Ebony agreed. 1953 came and Little Michael was two years old and Mitchell and Ebony began noticing his stranger behavior. Little Michael began staring at the walls with an angry look on his face, he would crawl to the Connor and close his eyes and a dark image would appear and vanish. When ever his parents would try to play with him he would just look at them with a blank found on his face and when ever his mother tried to feed him he would show no sentiment at all. Ebony then began to feel that something was seriously wrong with him so she took him to see her father for a prayer. When she arrived at her fathers Church he was sitting in the office with his deacons talking when Ebony and Little Michael knocked on the door. "Come in! Her father uttered! The Father looked at his grandson and asked Ebony what was wrong with him! Ebony then asked her father could they be alone to talk and the deacon got up and left the office. Ebony sat Little Michael on her lap and began telling him about his strange behavior and the father told her that she had to ask God for his forgiveness before he lift a finger to help her. Her father looked at Little Michael sitting on his her lap and seen that his eyes had a yellow glow inside and he began to back away. Then he looked at his daughter and yelled that her son was a spawn from hell and for her to get him out of his Church. Ebony looked at him in discuss and asked him why did he say that about his grandson, then she told him that he was the one that needed to ask God to forgive him. Then she got up and told him that he was the only spawn from hell not her son then she got up and left the Church cursing him under her breath. The Father ran to the door yelling to her that the Devil is hiding in her child's soul and that she should kill him while he is still young. Ebony began to cry as she walked out of the Church and Little Michael looked back at his grand father with a found on his face. Ebony went to the bus stop and waited until it came; when the bus arrived they got on it and as soon as the bus pulled away the Church exploded and her Father were burned to ashes. Ebony then became weak but then began feeling better, when she got home she called Mitchell and told him what her father had just done to them. Little Michael then stood up and walked over to the Television set and as he got closer the set turned on to the news. Ebony peeped in the living room and saw Little Michael standing up in front of the set watching it. She then told Mitchell that their son stood up and turned on the TV set and she walked over to him and hugged him. Then she saw on the news that her fathers Church had blew up and she stood their in shock as tears ran down her cheek. Mitchell began calling her but she would not answer, Ebony was in tears as she watched the coroners bring out her fathers dead body from the flaming Church. She then looked at Little Michael and saw that he was clapping his hand in enjoyment, she then softly whispered to Mitchell that Little Michael seem to enjoy that her father was killed in a fire. Mitchell yelled!" your father died! What the hell happen? Mitchell yelled out! Little Michael then sat back on the floor and stared at the TV and continued to clap his hands. Ebony looked at him with fear in her eyes and then turned and walked into the kitchen; she then sat down and continues to cry. That night when Mitchell got home he found Ebony fast asleep and Little Michael curled up next to her, Mitchell went into the Kitchen and fixed dinner and sat down and ate. Ebony woke up and went into the kitchen and seen that Mitchell was home and had fix his own plate, she then went into the living room and told Mitchell what happen with her and her father. After they finished talking they turned around and Little Michael was standing there looking at both of them with a strange look in his eyes. Ebony then looked at Little Michael and began getting scared, she then whispered to Mitchell that she felted that something was wrong with their son. Mitchell asked her what was he doing and she told him that he was watching the TV and clapping his hands, Mitchell began to feel the pain from her tears alone. As the tears ran down his face a strange screamed echoed from the back room, Ebony cried for a moment and then she began to feel like something negative left body. Mitchell then told Ebony to rest for the moment and she laid her head on him and closed her eyes. Mitchell then told Ebony to charm down and get some rest, and then he kissed and hugged her and told her that he loved her Ebony picked up her head and watched Little Michael crawl around. Little Michael crawled around for a few minutes then he looked at his mother and then crawled into the living room and began starring at the walls. Ebony went into the Kitchen and saw Little Michael starring at the wall but nothing was there, she wiped her eyes and picked him up and took him to the room and put him to bed. The next morning Mitchell got up and went to take a shower and he heard Ebony talking, he peeped to see who she was talking to but all he seen was her cooking Breakfast. Little Michael was stare at the wall; He kept seeing something looking at him. Ebony turned to give her son a smile but his attention was on the wall and Ebony looked at the wall to see what he was looking at but nothing was there. A strange face kept appearing and Little Michael was the only one that could see it and it seemed like it was talking to him. Ebony looked at Little Michael and asked him what was he looking at but he just starred at the wall with a blank look on his face. Little Michael kept seeing faces looking at him but he did not respond in any way. Ebony then turned towards the wall that he was looking at but did not see anything so she just went back to cooking, then Ebony realized that she had ran out of cooking oil so she had to go to the store. Ebony then went to her room and put on her coat, then she put on Little Michael jacket and took him with her to the neighborhood store. Mitchell had finished showering and got dress for work, he decided to get something outside and left. In the stone Ebony was pushing Little Michael in the shopping cart when she saw two white men in front of the counter staring at her. The two men began making racial comment towards her and her son, "I didn't know that they allowed spooks in markets! One of the men shouted out! For God sakes! Now the food is contaminated! The other white man yelled out! Then they both began laughing! Ebony just ignored them and walked pass them and as they walked towards the freezer area Little Michael looked at the two Men and smiled. One of the men told the other to look at the little monkey smiling and they began laughing even harder, Ebony went to the counter and paid for their food and left the store and as they walked out the door the lights began blinking off and on and a strong gust of wind came and sliced the two white men's heads clean off of their bodies. The blood covered the walls and floor of the store and the people inside began to panic in fear, when

Ebony and Little Michael got home she took off their coats then went back to the kitchen to finish cooking. She turned on the radio then went into the back to see was Mitchell still there but she seen that he left for work already, then she went back to the kitchen and looked in the ice box and took out a pack of pork chops to fix for dinner. Ebony then began feeling good and began singing along to it's a family affair by Sly and the family stone. Ebony was dancing and enjoying herself while the music was blasting out of the radio, Little Michael looked at his mother dancing and singing along to the radio when he turned and seen a strange face on the wall. Little Michael looked at the wall with a found on his face like he was about to cry but he did not, he just starred at it with a vacant look. Later that night Mitchell came in the door and announced that he was home and that the food smelled delicious, he went into the kitchen and gave his family a kiss and went into the bed room to get UN dress. Mitchell went into the bath room to take a shower and then he came out and sat down at the table and told Ebony about the day he had. He then told her in excitement that he made sixty bucks and he believes that more is coming. Then Ebony looked at Mitchell and told him that two racist men was insulting them when they were shopping and Mitchell became upset for the moment and told her that he would take care of it. Ebony fixed their plates and fed Little Michael, after dinner Mitchell took a walk to the store to find out who were the two men that disrespected his girl and child but when he arrived he found out that the two men had been killed. Mitchell went back to the apartment and told Ebony that the men was killed, then he picked up Little Michael and took him into the living room and began playing with him. While Ebony was washing dishes and thinking about the last words between her and her father! She began thinking about the crazy things her father had said about her son. Tears ran down the cheek of her face as she seen flash backs of the news reporting that her father was killed in a fire. Ebony then went into the living room and told Mitchell that she really started to feel bad about what father had said about Michael. Then she began feeling upset and then she started to cry that her father died hating his grandson, then Little Michael stopped and looked at his mother face, then he turned and looked at his father with a strange look. Mitchell told Ebony that he was sorry for her lost and maybe she should relax for the moment. He then got up and went into the kitchen and finished cleaning while Ebony sat down and watched TV, Little Michael turned and seen a face looking at him. Ebony then began to fall asleep when out of nowhere Michael yelled out in a dark demonic voice. "Stop looking at me" Mitchell then raced in the room also Ebony woke up and they both looked at Little Michael. Did you hear that Mitchell replied to Ebony! And she looked at Little Michael and became startled for a moment, and then Mitchell began to think about what the ghost said to him earlier. Ebony then told Mitchell that they must have been hearing things because Michael is only two years old and he can't speak yet. Mitchell agreed and they went back to what they were doing, Ebony then slowly walked over to Michael and picked him up, Little Michael just looked at her with a blank expression on his face. Ebony called Mitchell back to the living room and told him that she really thinks that something evil is controlling their son. Mitchell just looked at her and walked back to the kitchen, Ebony looked at Little Michael and mumbled to herself that it's wasn't fare! Mitchell then came back to the living room and told Ebony that their child is not possessed by anything and to just chill out. Ebony looked at Mitchell and told him that he may be right but Michael is acting weird for a child his age! Then she said you have to admit that at least. Mitchell looked at Little Michael and said my little king is special and that why he loves him so much. Ebony looked at Mitchell and asked him could they let one of the Church members say a prayer over Little Michael and Mitchell said ok. Mitchell then told Ebony that he feels that they should go to another Church because if their child is possessed her father did it to him. Ebony looked at him and walked away, Mitchell then went back to cleaning the kitchen and Little Michael just looked at them and smiled. Mitchell was in the kitchen saying that no God could create what he created and Little Michael eyes began to glow and the room began to get dark. Mitchell looked and seen what was happening and he became frightening and Ebony then raced out of the room asking what was going on and Mitchell replied that he did not know! The room began shaking and the lights were blinking off and on and strange voices were laughing and out of nowhere everything stopped and Little Michael was standing in front of them with his eyes full of flames. Mitchell looked into his sons eyes and uttered "God help us! Then he began to get spooked out and Little Michael eyes went back to normal, Mitchell looked at Ebony and they slowly approached him. Little Michael looked at his father and smiled then he reached out his hand for his father to pick him up and when Mitchell picked him up Little Michael touched his face and smiled. As the years passed Little Michael got older and his behavior got worst also his mother and father did their best to keep things under control. Finally Little Michael was the age to attend elementary school (P.S.35) on the dirtiest side of Avenue D in lower Manhattan. In School Little Michael never interacted with the children he just stood in the back of the class room starring at the walls. Little Michael also just sat at his desk drawing pictures of strange looking things, dolls with their heads cut off and little rabbits with horns. The teacher looked at his drawing and called his mother to ask her was their seriously something wrong with him. Ebony tried to explain to the teacher that Michael was a good child and she had nothing to worry about. Little Michael also use to draw pictures of ghostly souls burning and when the teacher showed Ebony it she just stood there in shock. The teacher felted that Michael's behavior would effect the other students in the classroom, the children were afraid to be near him. Ebony looked at the teacher and asked her did he ever hurt or attempt to hurt anyone and the teacher said no! Then Ebony asked the teacher to stop being predigested towards her child and just teach him. Ebony then went into the classroom and seen Little Michael in the back of the class talking to himself and stabbing the pencil into the desk. All of the children were backed up against the wall looking at Little Michael stab his desk and mumble to himself about pain. Ebony went over to him and picked him up and gave him a hug but all Michael did is staring at the other children with a blank look. Then out of nowhere Little Michael began screaming and hitting his mother in the face for no reason at all. The teacher and the children became very terrified behind Little Michael's behavior so they all ran to the right hand Connor of the classroom. Ebony began shaking Little Michael and then put him on the floor and he began laughing then his eyes rolled up in his head and then he pasted out. Then out of nowhere a loud demonic voice yelled out" (all must die and bow to me and then will I let this little boy free)! Ebony picked up Little Michael and he began to growl and shake then his body became very hot and she mistakenly dropped him and before he could hit the floor something grabbed him. Whatever grabbed him began shaking him and spinning him around in the air then he slammed to the floor and began screaming. The screams sounded like thousands of souls burning and then the cries stopped then his eyes opened up and he called for his mother. Ebony ran over and picked him up with tears running down her face and her heart pumping in fear for what she just witness. Ebony picked him up asked him was he alright but he just looked at her with a lost look on his face. Ebony hugged Little Michael and looked up and asked god to forgive her for leaving his house of worship, she then held him close to her heart and ask the lord to protect her son from all harm's way then she made a promise to return to Church and never leave again. Then he teacher came into the classroom with the principle and he asked her to come to his office to remove him from their school. Ebony did not try to fight in any way she just took her son and left, the principle told her to take Little Michael to a doctor and when he is better he can return to school. Ebony walked down the hall uttering to herself that Jesus will find a way for their family, as they were leaving the building Ebony heard the principle and the teacher calling Little Michael an evil spawn from hell. Tears ran down her face as she continued to say that it wasn't fare that this was happening to them. As they left the school and walked towards the bus stop Little Michael looked up and saw that his mother was crying and his eyes began to glow, he then looked back at the school and a strange black cloud appeared over the school. Inside the school the principle was in his office talking to a staff member when he began sweating heavily and little sparks of flames began appearing on his face. The principle began screaming and trying to take off his clothes but before he could get his shirt unhooked he burst into flames and burned to ashes. The other staff began bursting into flames, screaming to the top of their lungs, the teacher who called Michael a spawn from hell! Was in the class teaching the children how to spell when she began shaking and stuttering, then She let out a horrifying yell and exploded! Her blood and insides decorated the floor and walls. The children in the class all came running out covered with the teacher's blood and guts. The screams echoed through the air and the children all began to fall to the floor and breakout in huge blisters and their screams where heard outside. One of the other teachers saw the children in the hall on the floor screaming so she gathered them all together and lead them out of the school with the rest of all the children. As the faculty lead the rest of the children out of the building and up the block the building exploded! Ebony took Little Michael to the doctor for a checkup and found out that Little Michael had a double heart beat but the doctors could not find where the other heart beat was located. Little Michael looked at the doctor and began to found, The doctor looked at Little Michael and asked him what was wrong and Little Michael eyes began to glow, then the doctor fell into a deep trance and left the room saying that all. Then Ebony picked Little Michael up and left the doctors office and as soon as they got on the bus to go home the doctor pulled out a gun and began shooting everyone. Then after ward he turned the gun on his self and blew his brains out of his head, Ebony and Little Michael arrived home and she took off his coat then she went into the bed room to take off her coat to get relaxed. Ebony then came out of the room and went to the bath room to wash her hands then she went into the living room to wait until Mitchell got home from work. She was sitting on the sofa thinking how she was going to tell him about what took place at the school. Later that evening Mitchell came home with a big bag full of squirrel nuts and peanut chews for his family to snack on after dinner. Mitchell then went into the Living room and gave his women and their child a big kiss after doing so he sense that something was wrong. Mitchell looked at Ebony and seen that she was sad for some reason so he asked what was wrong and she told him to sit down. Mitchell placed his bag on the table and sat down next to her then she began telling him what she saw and Mitchell looked at her like she was losing her mind. Then she began to cry and told him that Little Michael was kicked out of school because they felt that he would put the other children in danger. He then looked at her and told her that everything was going to be alright then he gave her a kiss. Ebony then told him that they need Jesus in their life and everything would get worst if they did not get back into his house of worship. Mitchell looked at her and told her that the Church is what's causing all this mess between them. Then he pointed at their son and asked her how that handsome child could

could be possessed by anything! And then he told her that God would not let anything happen to their children. Mitchell then told Ebony that she had to stop letting the Church cloud her mind and just believe things will get better. Ebony sat there with tears in her eyes as Mitchell continued to babble about the Church brain washing her. Then he stop talking when he seen Little Michael looking at him with a strange found on his face, Mitchell then looked at Ebony and asked her what was his problem, then he looked at Little Michael and asked him did he understand what daddy was saying! Mitchell then picked up his bag and went to the bed room to get undressed, and then he went into the bathroom to take a shower. Later they were all sitting at the table having dinner when Mitchell looked at Ebony and told her that he would join the Church with her. Ebony then got up and hugged him, then telling him that she love him! Then she told Mitchell that she believes that God would work it all out for them. That night when Mitchell and Ebony was fast asleep some people were out in the hallway gambling and getting high, when Little Michael was awaken by the raucous in the hall, His eyes began to glow. Little Michael began to rise out of his bed and hovered out of the room and went through the front door then he floated down the stairs. Five men were in the hall shooting dice and smoking dust when

Little Michael appeared in front then with eyes full of flames. Then a voice rang out telling them that the time has come for them to burn in hell! The men looked at Little Michael and told him to get back in his house before he gets slapped up. Then Little Michael began whispering word in a strange language (eeema-dumah-kabee) and up the stairs came a strange black cloud appeared. The hall began getting hot and the men's bodies began smoking when they let out a horrifying yell and they burst into flame and burned into ashes. The screams echoed threw the air, people heard the screams but no one came out to see what happen. Little Michael then floated down stairs and seen two hookers having sex with a young man when Little Michael yelled out Nasty Flesh! You must die! And the two began melting away, the young man became frighten and pulled up his paint and ran towards the door. Before he could get outside the young man exploded, leaving his body part all over the floor, then a gust of dust mixed with the black cloud covered the front exit. Then Little Michael walked threw the strange black cloud and appeared the west village where he seen a gang of men beating on a young man. Little Michael floated towards them and his eyes began to glow, the men began to scream as their skin began pealing off of their bodies. As Little Michael stood there staring at them a dark image appeared in back of him and utter in a dark manner" You beat and push others around! Because he is gay you slap him around! Now it your turn to be laid down! The men all scattered with their bodies in flames, and then they fell on the ground leaving no remains. Then a dark cloud appeared and little Michael began to laugh, and then he vanished and appeared back in his bed fast asleep. The next day there were police officers in the hallway asking questions about what happen that night. One of the neighbors had saw a strange little boy in the hall ripping people to pieces and the neighbor told the officers that she believe he was from another planet. The alarm clock went off and Mitchell got up and went into the bath room to take a shower and Ebony ended up getting up shortly after then she went to fix breakfast for Mitchell before he went to work. Mitchell was in the shower blasting music and singing also Ebony as at the stove fixing grit, sausages and cheese eggs. Mitchell came out of the Shower and went to get dressed for work, then he came into the kitchen gave her kiss and sat down at the table. While the two was sitting at the table eating one of the officers knocked on the door and Mitchell got up and answered the door. One of the officers asked him did he hear anything in the hallway last night! Then he told Mitchell that five people were murdered in the hall, in the most horrifying way. Mitchell told the officer that neither he nor his family heard anything, and then he told him that people die in this dump every day, mostly by cops. Then he slammed the door in his face and went back to having breakfast with his women. Ebony got up from the table and went to see if Little Michael was up so that she could feed him also. Ebony was planning for Little Michael and her to spend a day together; she then went into the room and came out with Little Michael. Ebony sat him next to his father and went to fix Little Michael his plate and then she sat down to eat also. Mitchell rubbed the top of his little boys head and told Ebony that they are lucky to have such a handsome son. Little Michael began playing with his food and whispering to himself and Ebony turned to Mitchell and told him to watch his son having a conversation with the air. She then told Mitchell that Little Michael was very scary to other children his age and Mitchell told her that everything was going to be alright. Then Ebony told him that their son needs God in his life and Mitchell looked at her and told her that if going back to church will make her happy so be it. Then he wiped his mouth and got up from the table and went into the room to get dressed, and then he went back to the kitchen and gave them a kiss and walked out the front door. Ebony and Little Michael were sitting at the table eating when

Mitchell came back in the door claiming to have left something. Mitchell came into the kitchen and got down on one knee and asked Ebony for her hand in marriage then he pulled out a little decorated box. Ebony looked at it and tears ran down her cheek as she answered yes, Mitchell opened up the box and placed the ring on her finger. Little Michael looked at his father and began to shake, then a strong demonic voice uttered out" No! You are not going to marry that weak Christian dog! Her child molesting father is down here kissing little Demon's down here now! Then the voice yelled out that they were all dammed for life and no one turns their back on Satan! Then Little Michael fell to the floor and began yelling and screaming for help, Mitchell looked at Ebony in shock then he went to pick Little Michael up. But as Mitchell went to pick him up Little Michael became violent and began punching and clawing down Mitchell's face. Mitchell began to shake Little Michael until he pasted out in his arms and as he lay in his father's arm the voice told them that the child belonged to the Devil. Ebony and Mitchell put Little Michael to bed and called the neighborhood doctor, Mitchell called his job to inform them that he was not coming in tomorrow. Ebony and Mitchell waited until the doctor came and they watched him give Michael a checkup but he did not find anything wrong with him.

Mitchell told the doctor what Michael just said and the doctor say good day and left their home. Ebony then turned to Mitchell and told him that Little Michael needed Jesus and not a doctor and Mitchell looked in amazement and told her that they needed to find a Church. Mitchell and Ebony let the doctor out and they went to sit in the living room, they turned on the television and saw that the school Little Michael was kicked out from had burned down. Strangely the principle and the teacher were the only ones killed in the fire, Ebony's face turned as pale as a ghost and Mitchell looked puzzled. Ebony looked at Mitchell and said that it was strange that the school would burn down after what they did to him. Mitchell looked at her and asked her did she really think that their son was responsible for that tragedy, and then he told her that she was losing her mind and that she really needed to stop. Ebony told Mitchell that being that they left the Church God has took his hands off of them and their child is suffering for their stupidity, then she told him that she feels that he lost his faith and Mitchell replied that he lost it a long time ago. Ebony looked at him with sadness on her face, Ebony then told Mitchell that only faith in God could change things for them and Mitchell did not reply. Ebony cooked dinner and they sat down to eat and after dinner he went into the living room and continued to watch TV, The Jack Benny Show was on. Around 12:00 p.m. Mitchell had fell asleep with the set on and a few minutes later Little Michael came floating down the hall with his eyes glowing like the sun. Little Michael floated past the living room and threw the front door, then down the hall and down the stairs. A bunch of gang members where hanging in the front of the building when Little Michael came floating out of the lobby door. What the Hell! One of the gang members yelled out! Little Michael froze in his tracks and stared at him and said" Hey punks! Where is your nasty mother hiding? I need some company! Then he began laughing in a wicket manner! The gang member got upset and threw a punch at Little Michael and by the time his fist reached Michael's face he had turned into a strange creature and attacked and killed all of them. The beast began tearing the flesh off of each of them, ripping then to shreds and their screams echoed threw the sky, after that Little Michael began killing and feeding on everyone he became in counted with. This weird looking beast ran down the street attacking and eating people, leaving nothing but blood and bones. After viciously killing and eating over thirty people, he finally made his way back home. The time was 2:30 a.m. in the morning and Little Michael came floating threw the door, and then he floated back into his parents room and fell right asleep. The next morning Mitchell woke up and found Little Michael sitting up watching them, Mitchell got up and walked over to his little boy and smiled. How is my little boy? Mitchell asked! Then he gave him a kiss on the fore head! Little Michael smiled and lay back down and closed his eyes. Mitchell looked at his son and uttered to himself that his son is a blessing send from Heaven, then as he stared at his son he began to hear a voice say that him and his son will come to war. Mitchell looked around to see where that voice was coming from, but he did not see anything. Ebony woke up shortly and saw Mitchell looking at their child and she smiled, then he turned and told his wife that no matter what her father said or anyone say Little Michael is a blessing. Ebony looked at Mitchell and told him that they needed God in their life and that she was going back to Church with or without him. Mitchell told her that he would go back with her, and then he told her to find a Church! Then he told her that his faith was not strong but he would give it a try once more. Then the two joined a local Church on the other side of the neighborhood, Ebony began to feel much better that she had came back into the Lords house again. Mitchell tried to tell him self that he did not need Church but end up getting caught up in the word and he began getting up lifted again. Ebony's mother was the sweet heart that invited then back to the Lords house and at the time she was the acting Minister. While sitting in the serves' a little old lady walked into the Church claiming to be looking for Lucifer's son. Everyone in the neighborhood seen the old lady before but she never bothered anyone, she was a sweet elderly women who like to feed birds in the park. The Little old lady name was Haddi Freemont and everyone seem to like her in the neighborhood, but she had a son name Jesse, that had a problem with his attitude. Jesse was a mean and negative sprit person; all he did was walk around making bad comments about how people looked and act. Nothing was ever good enough for him; he complained about how nice his mother was and how she made him sick. Jesse only went to work and came home; no one wanted to be bothered with him because he was always saying something negative. So the people were surprise to hear Miss Haddi speaking about looking for Lucifer's son, they wouldn't have been surprise if he was the one worshiping the Devil. People looked around as Miss Haddi walked up and down the aisle's calling for the young Master to send her to Hell. Then she arrived to the aisle where the Robinson Family was sitting and she kneeled down, and then screamed in a high pitched voice. "All Hail the Prince of Evil! Then she pulled out a knife and asked Little Michael to plunge it into her heart! Mitchell stood up and told to get her bugged out behind away from his family. Then the ushers came and removed her from the Church and as soon as she walked up the block a piece of metal fell out of the sky and cut her in half, sticking in the ground. As Haddi's body fell apart it burst into flames then exploded, all that was left was a blood stains in the shape of a person. On the Connor was a young man screaming at the top of his lungs that the anti Christ was here and the end of the world have finally come. Nothing good came out of his mouth; he began yelling out that black people are too Black and White people are too White. Then he began screaming at people and telling them that there are no real jobs out here, then he began screaming that there are too many people on the earth. Then he began saying that God hates offends and gays and out of no where an old man appeared and shot him in the head. Then the old man stood up and walked over to him and yelled out that God hates him also, and then he disappeared. Mean while in the Church the Minister began telling the congregation that the Devil poisons the minds of the UN righteous. As the Minister was preaching Mitchell heled his son close and kissed his wife, telling them that it's ok. After Servest was over everyone began leaving the building and as they walked out side they all seen the blood stain of old lady

Haddi. The people from the Church just stood there calling to the Lord for protection and as the Robinsons walked out the sky became dark. Mitchell and his wife looked up and asked them self what was going on and as soon as the words left their mouth the sky opened up. It began thundering and poring down, the people began running to there cars as the Robinson's fell into a trance and Little Michael's eyes began to glow. The Church doors slam shut and the rain began turning into flames, the people in the street began yelling and screaming as the flames attached to their bodies. "The world is ending! The people yelled as they fell to the ground calling for God to help them. Then a strange misty cloud covered the Robinson's as they made their way home, The Robinson caught a cab to the house and awoke from the trance they were in. The Robinson sat at the dinner table and began talking about what happen at church and why did that bugged out lady bow down to their child. Ebony looked at Little Michael and smiled, and then Mitchell looked at his son and told Ebony that too much weird things happen in Church today. He then told her that maybe they should find another Church to go too and Ebony looked at him and said "are you afraid of a bugged out old lady? Then she asked him was he worried that she might gum him to death! They both started to laugh; they both went back to eating! Little Michael stopped eating and looked at them both and something was telling him to kill them both, but Little Michael was resisting it, he kept shaking his head no! The voice then told him that he belonged to the Devil and not them. After dinner Mitchell picked up his son and took him to the room and laid him on the bed and began talking to him. Little Michael looked at his father and began to smile, then Mitchell began feeling strange, he began seeing visions of a weird man trying to kill his son. He kept seeing this vision and it began to bother him so he looked at his son and told him that he will always protect him no matter what. Then he looked up to the Heavens and asked God to give him the straight to protect his family no matter how hard it might be. Then he turned to his son and smiled as his little boy fell asleep, then Mitchell went to bed and told his wife that he feel that someone wants to hurt his family. That night Jesse was sitting in a bar drinking, he began talking about there being Demons on the earth and the head Demon has come to seek and destroy. That all he talks about when he was in the presents of others, everyone that came in contact with him ended up leaving angry. Around 2:30 in the morning Jesse was trying to hale down a cab when a strange man appeared next to him and then disappeared. Jesse turned around in fear but began to realize that maybe he was just seeing things, the cab came and he went home, That morning around 5:30 a.m. Jesse was awaken by a large rumbling sound from a garbage truck. Oh Lord! Oh Lord! That sickening garbage truck again! Jesse yelled out! What the heck is wrong with these dumb city workers? Can they find some where else to make there freaking noise then he looked at the clock. Oh butt! I am late! Let me get out of here, and then he jumped up and put on his clothes then ran out of the apartment. He caught a cab up the block and got to the job, the boss just looked at him as he rushed in and just caught the driver as he was about to leave with someone else. The other person got out of the truck and went with another driver, as they drove off Jesse began complaining about how his job sucks and he began calling the boss a big fat happy meal. The driver just ignored him not uttering a word to him but he just kept complaining, then he looked at the driver and seen that he was not paying him any attention. Then he crossed his arms and uttered to himself that he wished everybody around him just drop dead. The driver just glanced at him shaking his head then Jesse climbed into the back of the truck and lift up the back door tossing the papers in front of the stores. 8 a.m. came and the driver drove back to the job, Jesse jumped out and punched out and left. Jesse was standing at the bus stop when he seen the others going to the Restaurant for breakfast but nobody asked him to come. Jesse looked at them with a hurt look but yelled out that he didn't give a rams butt! But the workers just ignored him and went to eat. The bus finally came and Jesse got on it calling his co-workers a bunch of phony fart sniffers and he looked at the bus driver and called him a clown. Then he walked to the back to find some where to sit down, an elderly man was sitting in the back seat with his eyes closed. Jesse rudely pushed the man leg out the way and went to sit down near the window; the elderly man just glanced at him and closed his eyes again. Jesse then began cursing out people on the bus for looking at him then he yelled out that he wish he was all alone and the elderly man whispered" be careful what you wish for it just might come true! Jesse looked at the elderly man and told him to mind his dam business and the man's eyes opened. Jesse seen that the eyes where pure black so he pulled the stop string to get off the bus. The elderly man stood up and Jesse rush to get off the bus and as he was getting off he looked back and the elderly man wasn't there only a middle age girl reading. Jesse wasn't to far from his area so he walked the rest of the way but as he was walking home things on the street was disappearing before his eyes. Jesse stopped and seen the streets becoming empty as he pass by it, he then began seeing visions of Little Michael smiling at him with his eyes glowing. Jesse finally arrived at the project were he lived and began seeing everything disappear in front of him, the people and the building began disappearing and re-appearing in front of him. Jesse began rubbing his eyes and asking him self "what was going on! Then everything re-appeared and he continued. As he began walking to the building it seems kind of strange because people walked passed him like he wasn't there. No one ever looked his way it seemed like he was invisible to the human eye, he looked at people and waved at them but they just walked past him. When he got to his building he went in and went upstairs then he went inside the apartment. Jesse then yelled out" there's nothing on the stove and he turned to the wall and picked up an empty pot and showed it. Then the ghost of his dead mother appeared and pointed at him and told him that he had to kill the Demon seed. Jesse just looked at the ghost with a dumb grin on his face, and then he yelled out "mom! Where's my freaking food! Jesse then went into his room to change for school but he went to eat first. Around 10:45 a.m. Jesse left the apartment and went to catch the bus to school and was confronted by the elderly man he meets on the bus. The elderly man looked at him and asked him was he always freaking crazy, and then he asked him did he believe in God. Jesse looked at the old man and said No! And yes! Yes he believes in God and no! He is not crazy! Then the elderly man walked away and yelled out that he is still a sick fool! Then he turn towards Jesse and said "you have to be sick to face what you are about to face son! It's Evil! Pure Evil! Jesse looked at the elderly man as he walked away and called him an old dusty boot! Jesse then waved his hand at the elderly man and went to school, around lunch time when Jesse was on his way to the cafeteria he began seeing people walking in a trace, what the heck is going on? Jesse asked! As the people walked pass him with a blank look on their faces! Then when he sat down to eat a young girl came up to him with her eyes glowing! Jesse turned to her and screamed! Oh my! What happen to your freaking eyes? Jesse yelled out in fear! The young girl grabbed his face and told him that his boot sniffing mother needs his company in Hell. Jesse jumped up and pushed the young girl off of him and began running towards the door when the whole cafeteria stood up and started chasing him down the hallway. Jesse was screaming for help but it seemed like the whole school was out to kill him! The Master wants your soul! The people in the school yelled out! Fear filled Jesse's heart as he made his way to the exit door. But when he reached the out side Little Michael was standing there holding his Mothers hand with both of their eye's glowing like the sun. Jesse screamed! As Little Michael let go of his Mother's hand and began turning into a strange looking creature, Jesse tried to turn and run back into the school when Little Michael leaped on to his back and began ripping into his back. As his claws tore threw his clothes it began tearing pieces of flesh, Jesse's body began to bubble from the heat as Little Michael began biting into him. As the blood pored from his body the beast began drinking it and Jesse fell to the ground calling for his mother to help him. The Beast jumped off of him and the doors of the school opened up and Beast ran inside and began killing everything in his path. All you heard was screams of terror, bones cracking and sounds of tearing flesh everywhere, and when the doors opened up a river of Blood ran down the stairs. Little Michael came walking out covered in blood and holding a arm in his hand, his mother walked up to him and grabbed his hand and they both disappeared. That evening when Mitchell came home he found Ebony and Little Michael sitting at the table in a trance. What's up baby? Mitchell asked! Ebony and Little Michael just stared at each other with blank looks on their faces. Mitchell went over to them and grabbed and shook his wife until she woke out of the trace. A few minutes later Little Michael woke up and got up and walked to the back room and closed the door behind him. Years passed and Little Michael grew older and older and unsolved murdered continue to happen all over town, the people in the area began to live in much fear of the Robinson family. On Little Michael's fourteenth birthday the area became more fearful of Little Michael because of the prediction about the son of the Devil will come into power of the people. That Monday at school Little Michael was sitting in his class room and the teacher was teaching the class about History. The teacher then began asking question and Little Michael began answering it correctly before the teacher could finish. The other Children in the class became very envious towards Little Michael's intelligence; Little Michael was very solf spoken person and never bothered any one. In the class was a bully name Ronald, the whole class feared him because of his older brother who was the leader of a notorious biker gang called the Death Riders! Ronald decided to use his brother's reputation to bully on Little Michael because of his intelligence, he then balled up a piece of paper and spit on it and threw it at Little Michael's head. Then he yelled out that he would see him after school and Little Michael turned to him and smiled and said he will be there. After school Little Michael waited in the school yard for Ronald to come out, a few minutes later Ronald came out with four of his friends and they walked up to Little Michael! What's up mud face? Ronald yelled out! Little Michael just looked at him smiling! Then Ronald shouted out" do you thinking I am joking with you? Then he threw a punch and hit Little Michael in the face. Little Michael's eyes began to glow and the people that was out there all fell into a trance. Ronald and his friends started screaming and calling for their mothers as their skin began to bubble and peeling off of their bodies. Somebody Help me! The boys yelled out as their flesh began falling to the ground and their blood began getting effected from their clothes fabric. The more they screamed for help, the less the people heard, No one moved a muscle! They just stood there in a mummified state of mind. As their flesh began to burn the boys yelled out to God asking him to save them and Little Michael looked at them and begging for their lives so he turns away and left. The skin of the boys returned then the pain stopped and the boys ran home crying, Ronald yelled out that he was going to bring his brother to kill him and Little Michael stopped in his tracks and looked at him smiling. Little Michael's mother showed up shortly and she took him home, Little Michael told his mother that the children in this world has a lot to learn about respect. Then he told her that the boys in is class wanted to beat him up but he stood his grounds. Ebony asked Little Michael to sit at the table so that they could have a talk; she then told him that he had to learn to ignore people. Little Michael smiled at his mother and walked into his room, Ebony took off her coat and started dinner, Mitchell later came home and Ebony told him that their son was almost in a fight. Mitchell asked was he alright! And Ebony replied that he was fine but she was really worried about the other children in the school that bothered him. Ebony went back to cooking dinner while Mitchell went to talk to Little Michael about what happen at school today. Little Michael told his father that the little boys in the school thinks that he is weak and can not protect him self, He then told his father that he almost lost his cool and hurt them badly. Mitchell looked at his son and then told him that it wasn't worth it and the children that were bothering him wasn't properly trained by their parents. Late that night when Ebony and Mitchell was asleep, Little Michael was lying in his bed thinking when a strange shadow appeared on the wall and it turned into a strange looking dog. The eyes began to glow and Little Michael began to shake and foam from the mouth, his eyes rolled up in his head and when it came back down his eyes were flaming red. Little Michael's body rose up and he disappeared and he appeared at the park where the Demon riders hung out. The biker group was hanging around a garbage can of fire smoking and drinking, Ronald and his older Brother Shadow were talking. The flames enhanced and Little Michael appeared out of the fire and turned into a large Wolf type Creature and he attack the whole gang ripping and tearing them to pieces. Shadow grabbed his little brother and put him on the back of his bike and road off! Ronald looked back and began screaming that the Devil was out to kill them and that's the little boy that attacked him in school. The beast chased them down for miles until he found the right moment and he leaped and snatched Ronald from off of the back seat and began feeding on him. Ronald was screaming as the beast fangs dug into his flesh and he began ripping out chunks. Shadow heard his little brother screaming and he turned the bike around, then his road towards the beast screaming! As he drew closer the beast leaped and bit off his head, the body and bike smashed into another car and it exploded. After eating Ronald, Little Michael turned back to him self and disappeared. The next day when Little Michael was at school, the school teacher was telling the class how it was all over the news about Ronald and his brother being killed. The whole class looked shocked but Little Michael, he just smiled and went back to reading. After school Little Michael was standing in the school yard waiting for his mother to arrive, when some of Ronald's friend came out of the school and him standing there so they ran. A few minutes later the boys came back with a police officer and told him that Little Michael was the creature that Killed Ronald and his brother. The officer looked at Little Michael and looked back at them and walked away shaking his head. The Little boys pointed at him and called him a Devil and ran off, Little Michael looked at him smiled. The boys took off and Little Michael looked at their left leg and it began to grow weak until it gave out, then the boys fell to the ground. A big dark cloud appeared then covered to boys and all you heard was screams. Ebony arrived at the school and Little Michael was in the yard laughing when his mother walked up to him and asked what was so funny and Michael told her that the little boys called him the Devil. Ebony looked at her son and asked him were those boys still bothering him? And Michael told her that he had it in control. After that they walked to the bus stop and went home, when the two got home Little Michael began feeling strange and his body became over heated. Little Michael began feeling different; he began feeling like some powerful force had taking over his body and soul. A change has began in Little Michael's life, the Evilness has began to spread threw him and he was find with it. Ebony looked at Little Michael and asked him was he alright and he looked at her and said that he never felt better in his life. Then Little Michael went into the Bathroom and looked in the mirror and saw himself looking stronger. His eyes were pitch black and it change back to normal then he seen a reflection in the mirror of the Devil. The Devil looked at him and told him that he would one day sit beside him in Hell as second ruler and Little Michael smiled. Years began to past and people in the neighborhood began to strangely disappear and no one had a clue to how and what happen. Over 500 hundred teens turned up missing threw out the years and no one found a single trace of them anywhere. All they found was bones and blood where the people where missing from. Drug dealers, Drug addicts, Hustlers, Hookers ended up missing from the neighborhood also people from the Police department turned up missing also. As the years pasted the area drew worst and Little Michael grew meaner and meaner, Ebony and Mitchell grew older and became more involved in the Church and Little Michael began hanging with the wrong type of people. Little Michael was a teenager in Junior high School and he was getting into lots of trouble, he became the ring leader of a little cult call Hells Children. Little Michael's trust for Evil grew stronger and stronger until he became totally drunk with power. He began controlling the teacher's minds to give him and his friend's good grades even when they would cut school. After school Little Michael and his Friends would hang on the block starting trouble with people for no reason at all. The neighborhood became dark and gloomy when stores also people began getting robed by teenage kids. Little Michael and his friends began terrorizing the area and everyone in it, the neighborhood gangs all got together to try to stop them but failed drastically. The next day the community all gathered in the neighborhood center with the officers from the Prescient. People were complaining about the killing and Evil things that was going on in the neighborhood. The sergeant told the people that they were concern about the crazy things that was happening also to there officer as well. The people began screaming to the top of their lungs for justice to be served and that they should rage war a pond them. Ebony was sitting the crowd when she heard the people yelling for her child's head but she did not know that her son was involved. Out side across the street Little Michael was walking pass a grocery store and saw a cashier counting money so he and his friend went in and robed the man and killed him. After brutally killing the cashier he marked the fore heads of the others and filled their soul with the demonic sprits. The children eyes began to glow and they started changing into strange looking creatures, then went back to normal. They all walked out of the store with their eyes in flames, as they walked down the block, the people around them began dropping to their knees. Little Michael turned and looked at them and they two became Demons walkers. Little Michael then decided to call it a night, he then told the others to bring more people to Satan and they all agreed! He then disappeared and re-appeared in his room, no one was home yet! But a few minutes later Mitchell and Ebony walked in the front door. Were home! Mitchell yelled out! And Little Michael came out of his bedroom pretending that he had just got finish studying. What's up! How was the meeting? Michael asked! Ebony told him that there is a strange bunch of boys walking around killing people for no reason and drinking their blood, Mitchell then told him that he had to be careful out there! Michael looked at him and told him that he was not worried at all. Mitchell looked at him strange and Little Michael turned and walked into his room. Ebony shouted out is you hungry and Michael said that he already ate, and Ebony looked at Mitchell and said that Michael has been acting strange lately. Mitchell stared at her and told her that something was Evil about their son! And he can feel it every time he is near them. Then he told her that his appearance has change drastically and he does not look like a Robinson anymore. Ebony pulsed for a moment and said that his head has enlarged a bit plus he is much darker. Mitchell then told her about the time he seen a sprit and it told him that one day he would have to killing his own son and Ebony told him that she had that feeling the day he was born. Then they looked at each other and chuckled and said that that was non sense. Ebony then went to fix dinner and Mitchell went into the bathroom to take a shower. Later that night when Ebony and Mitchell were in the Living room watching Television, they began reminiscing about the day they first met, and also the day that Little Michael was born. Mitchell looked at his wife and told her that he feels that Evil has taken residents in their house hold and Ebony agreed. Ebony looked at Mitchell and asked what was they going to do about it and Mitchell grabbed her hand and told her lets pray! They both closed their eyes and began asking the Lord for guidance and peeping around the Connor of the living room door was Little Michael with anger in his eyes. The next morning Little Michael had got up and left for school when he was greeted in front of his building by a strange pale black man with an afro. What's up Little Michael! The strange man asked! And Little Michael turned and looked at him and said" who the are you? You weird looking freak; the man smiled and said"

Your worst nightmare if your not careful of what you say to me. Then he grabbed him up by his neck and looked him in the eyes and Little Michael began screaming! Then the strange man slammed him to the ground and then he looked at him and repeated" What's up Little Michael? Little Michael rolled over and bowed to the strange man and said "I am good Master! The strange man then told him to stand and told him that it was time to know the truth. He then told Little Michael to walk with him and he did so without uttering a word, the strange man told him how his family member made a Deal with the Devil for his soul. Little Michael looked at him and asked him who was it that made that deal and the Strange man told him not to worry but he is the chosen one to rule Hell on earth. The man then told him that he would be a great ruler and even God is going to tremble to his feet. Little Michael started to smile and the strange mans eyes began to glow and then he disappeared and Little Michael did also. He re-appeared in front of his school yard threw a ball of flames, when he stepped out people in the area drew weak. Little Michael went inside the school and too his classroom, the Teacher asked him why was he late but Michael never said a word. Little Michael sat down at his desk and stared at the teacher then he began whispering strange words and the teacher fell down to his knees then screamed out Oh! God! Help me! Then he exploded! Then Little Michael turned and looked at the rest of the class with his eyes in flames. The children in the class jumped out of their seats and began running for the door but Little Michael disappeared and re-appeared out side of the door and locked them in it then the room busted into flames and all the children in the class were buried. The Principle came out of his office and saw Little Michael holding the door while the children were screaming! He yelled out" what are you doing? And Little Michael turned and turned the Principle into a lump of poop. Then he looked at the students while they burned and smiled, then he walked away feeling no regrets so ever. He then walked out of the school laughing when a bunch teenager walked up to him and then began to bow. You are the choosing one! Then they fell to the ground and called him Master! Little Michael smiled and told them to rise, and then he told them that he needed to bring pain to those who deserve it. A large ball of fire appeared and Little Michael and his new group of friends walked threw it and appeared in front of a biker group's club house. Two big bikers was at the door standing guard at the door when Little Michael and his boys walked up to the front door and the bikers asked then were was they going? Little Michael looked at the bikers and told him that he heard that his mothers was in there giving free head! The Biker looked at Little Michael and told him that Negros die for less! And if he says another word, he is going beat the tar off of his watermelon eating butt. Little Michael looked at the other biker and he pulled out his gun and shot his partner in the head, then he opened up the door and Little Michael and his friends turned into strange looking wolf like creatures, then they ran into the club and murdered everyone in the club house. After the screaming and gunfire stopped! Little Michael and his friends came walking out covered in blood. Little Michael looked at the biker at the door and the bike put the gun to his temple area and pulled the trigger. They each walked out holding an arm of a different biker, then a big ball of flames appeared and they walked into it and disappeared. That evening; Little Michael was standing in front of his building with his new hangout buddies when they seen an old drunk man talking to himself about the Devil being on the earth and how he was a ugly mother sucker. Little Michael heard that and walked up to the old man and spat in his face and the rest of his friends began pushing around the elderly man. Later that evening Mitchell came home and saw them pushing around the elderly homeless man. He then ran over to him and asked him what he was doing! And Little Michael looked at his father and told him that he was cleaning up the trash. Then Little Michael told his Father that the old fool insulted him also that dirty clown like that shouldn't be allow to live. Mitchell grabbed him and dragged him to the building, "What's wrong with you boy? I raised you better then that! Mitchell uttered! We brought you up better then that, he is an elderly person and you know better! Mitchell shouted! The he told Little Michael that he has been acting weird lately and being very disrespectful to people. Little Michael looked at his father with a silly grin on his face and told him that he was sorry! Mitchell looked at his son and told him that sense he been hanging with those low life's he has become some what evil in peoples eyes. Then he told Little Michael that he needs God in his life and that he needed to return to Church. Mitchell then looked at his son and told him that he needed to ask the lord for forgiveness and Little Michael looked at his father and yelled" For what! Being burn! Then he looked at his father with anger in his eyes; Then Little Michael said in a low spoken tone, "the hell with Church and your fairly Preacher! Then he looked at his father and told him that the Preacher is getting hit off by the Deacon in the Church. Then he smiled at his father and told him that his father raped their mother in the Church. Mitchell looks at him with a strange look on his face and began to back away. Then Little Michael looks at his Father and told him that the Devil is his real father and thank you for raising him so well. Then Little Michael turn and went upstairs laughing as Mitchell just stood there staring. A few minutes later Mitchell came up stairs and walked in the door like he had just seen a ghost, ebony looked at him and asked him what was wrong but he didn't say anything he just walked into the bedroom. Ebony came into the room and Mitchell was sitting on the bed with his he down crying, Ebony came in and hugged him. "What the matter honey? Ebony asked! Mitchell looked at Ebony and told her that the vision he had about their son was true! She looked at him and asked him what he was talking about and the about the spirit that came to him when Little Michael was born. Then he told her that the spirit told him that Little Michael was Evil and one day he would have to kill him and Ebony's face turned pale. Then he looked at Ebony and asked her did his father even force himself on her when she was young in the Church! Ebony looked at him and began crying! How did you know that! She asked! A blank look appeared on his face. He then looked at her and told her what happen down stairs and that Michael told him that his father raped you in the church also that the Devil was his real father. Ebony looked at him with fear in her eyes and told him that she had a similar in counter about Little Michael also. After a while of weeping they finally came out of the room and went into the Kitchen, where Little Michael was sitting at the table smiling. Ebony went to the stove and began cooking while Mitchell sat at the table across from Little Michael. Little Michael looked at his father and Mitchell just crossed his arms then began to shake his head. Little Michael asked his father was he ok and he said yes he was ok and Michael told him that they had nothing to fear from him. Mitchell looked at him and told him that God protects him and that he wasn't worried at all, Little Michael smiled and said ok pop and got up from the table then went into his room. Months began to past and the Robinson faith began to get stronger but Little Michael drew further apart from his family and began getting into a lot of trouble with the law. Little Michael became the biggest and the most notorious gang leader in the hood, the people on the street feared him. At first all the riff raffs began disappearing from the area, then the thugs and the dealers began disappearing also, then the police began feeling the wrath of Little Michael and his worshipers. A blood bath rained on the lower east side of Manhattan, the news reporters reported a pack of wild wolf like creatures were ripping and tearing people to pieces. Years began to pass and the Robinson began the build the strength to do god will and destroy Little Michael.

Mitchell became the Bishop of the Church and Ebony was the first lady and the Church members grew larger in numbers. The faith in God grew stronger because of all the strange killings that accrued threw out the years, and as their faith grew so was the power in them grew also. Bishop Mitchell told the Church that the Devil possessed his son told him away from him and the Lord will give him the sign when he will get him back. The Church cheered and told the Bishop that they were ready to go into battle with him and help seen those Demons back to hell in Holy Ghost body bags. That night some people were walking in the streets making their way to work and in a nearby park was a pack of wolf like creature staring at them from the darkness in the park. As the people walked past the park they began to hear growls and before they could do anything the wild beast like creatures leaped out and tore them to pieces. They then began to turn back into human being; Little Michael stood up and told the others to get ready for war. As they stood over the slaughtered bodies the young boys began to change into demons as they stood up, Little Michael kicked the bodies to the side and looked at each and every one of them and told them that the master is on his way. They all let out a horrifying yell and turned back into Wolves then they ran off, the time was getting late and Little Michael went up stairs. Mitchell and Ebony were sitting at the kitchen table when Little Michael walked in, do you know what time it is? Mitchell asked! Michael looked at him and walked into his room, Mitchell stood up and went to the room and told Little Michael that if he couldn't respect their home that he needed to leave. Little Michael looked at him and said that he was out and don't end up being a Holy fairy like his mentor, then he asked his father to have a good life and he walked out. As he headed for the front door Ebony looked at him and told him that he was dead wrong and Little Michael looked at her and said that he know! As he opened up the door he looked at his mother and told her that maybe now he would have the guts to kill him when the time comes. Then he walked out the door and disappeared, Ebony and Mitchell looked out the door and was gone. Mitchell closed the door and Ebony looked at him and Mitchell looked at her and said that Evil must leave their home for God to dwell inside. They went back into the kitchen then sat down at the table and began to talk about what was about to come. Ebony Looked at her husband and told him that she was frightened and told her that he was also. Out side of the building Little Michael sat on the bench looking up in the sky and said" if you really do exist and you are God, Give my father the straight to kill me! I never ask for this! Then out of the shadows a strange man appeared, there is no God! Little man! Only me! I am your God and no one is more powerful then me, then he touched Michaels fore head and his eyes turned black. The strange man looked at Michael and told him that no one will survive this time and he raised his hand and a ball of fire appeared and they both walked threw it. An hour later they ended up in front of a Church was the Bishop is a fornicator! He was married and sleeping with little teenage girls at the same time! The Strange man told him. So the strange man asked Little Michael how should they be punished and Little Michael smiled and said these mother suckers should burn! The strange man lifted up his cane and the whole Church busted into flames and every one ran out in flames burning to ashes. They disappeared and ended up in Queens at a Church in Jamaica, where the Bishop was messing with the little boys in Bible class. Little Michael looked at the strange man and asked him what should be done to the Bishop of this Church? And the strange man looked at Little Michael said it is your call! And Little Michael looked back at him and said tic for tack, Let someone pop him right back! And the strange man said so be it! And he rose up his cane and the doors of the Church flung open and the strange man whispered something. A strange red mist appeared over the men in the Church and they all got up out of their seats and attacked and beat the Bishop. As the men in the Church was attacking the Bishop he began screaming for help the men began yelling was my little boy saying that when you was doing this to him? The men were hitting him with long Sharpe objects on his back and head, and then they kicked him in the mouth until the Bishop passed out and died. The women in the Church began screaming and calling for Jesus! Little Michael appeared over the pull pit and told the people that they call out a name that they don't respect. Then he pointed at the dead Bishop and said" This flaming fairy raped and molested your little boys and you still follow him? Now you act like you didn't know! Your punishment is death! Then he looked at the children and their parents and they became paralyzed in their seats. They began screaming and Little Michael disappeared and the Church exploded and all of the parents burned to ashes. But the children strangely disappeared and Little Michael and the strange man felt it, a weakness came over them because all of the souls were not delivered. The strange man looked to the heavens and yelled out" They were mine! Dam you! And ball of flames appeared and they jumped threw it. That morning, Mitchell and Ebony were sitting at the table eating when the door bell rang and strange looking women stood in front of the peep hole. Mitchell got up and went to the door and asked who is it and the person on the other side replied that she was sister Notbooger from first Christ Temple. Mitchell opened up the door and the strange looking women looked at him and told him that if he believed in God, he was a fool! Then she hawked green slime in his face and disappeared. Mitchell wiped his eyes and tried to grab the women but she had disappeared. Mitchell opened his eyes and looked down the hallway and screamed "come back here you Demon! Then he slammed the door and went to wash his face in the bathroom, Ebony then ran over to him and asked what happen! He then told her that a strange looking woman told him if he believes in God he is a fool and then spat in his face then ran off. Mitchell then became enraged and started to call to the lord for guidance when he began feeling funny inside his body. Then Mitchell went into the bedroom and put on his coat and told his wife that he was going to the Church to pray. Outside Little Michael was hanging with his new clan of followers when he saw his Father come out of the Building yelling to him self. Little Michael looked at him as he walked off angry, Little Michael wondered what had happen to him to get his father's anger so flared up so he followed him from a distance. His father walked to the Church up the block and as Little Michael drew closer to the Church he began feeling weak. He then stopped in his tracks and began hearing his father complaining about an elderly women hawking in his face. Little Michael looked up and began to think who would do that to him, then the strange man appeared next to him and told him that they had more work to be done. Little Michael looked at the strange man and asked him about the elderly women that spit in his fathers face and the strange man laughed. The strange man lifted up his cane and a big ball of fire appeared and they walked threw it and it disappeared. The Ball of flame re-appeared in front of a home on the top of a hill in the South Bronx. In the home was a family called the Madison's who inherited the land and home from their grand parents. The family moved from the Deep South and settled in the South Bronx, the Father was a well known Preacher from the South who was ran off because no nonsense rules against Satan. The strange man accused the Preacher for forcing himself on little girls in the neighborhood. Little Michael looked at the Preachers home and saw him having dinner with his family. Little Michael became out raged and told the strange man that the Preacher was a dog and he feel that sense he feels its alright to touch little girls, so it be the same for his kids! Then the strange man held up his cane and a pack of wild dogs appeared and ran towards the Preachers front door and broke threw it and jumped on the Preachers two daughters and had their way. The Preacher tried to get the dogs off of his children but the wild dogs turn into creatures and attacked and killed everyone in the house hold. As the screams echoed threw the air Little Michael grew stronger and you could see the souls of the murdered victims leaving the home and going into the strange mans cane. The big ball of Flame appeared and they walked threw it and ended up front of a cheap hotel in Brooklyn, the people living in the place was using drugs, dealing drugs, and prostituting so the strange man said. Little Michael looked at the strange man and asked him what happen to his father! The strange man just looked at him and told him not to ask him not to ask him any questions, Little Michael looked at him with rage in his face. The Strange man pulsed for a moment, and then he looked at him and said "anytime you feel like jumping, just go for it! Little Michael looked at the strange man and saw fire burning in his eyes and became scared. He then asked Little Michael how should these sinners's die and he then said make it fast and quick! Then the strange man let out a yell! Then the strange man lifted up his cane and the hotel began to shake, and then it exploded. The explosion was so intense that the souls of the people came screaming out of the burning Hotel and it ended up in the strange man's cane. Little Michael looked at the strange man and told him that he didn't want anything to happen to his parents and the strange man told him that all is damned. Then he looked at Little Michael and told him that his parent is going to try to kill him when he gets twenty one years of age. Little Michael yelled that he was a liar and his parents wouldn't do that to him and the strange man told him to look into the crystal on his cane. Little Michael looked at the crystal and the image of an angel telling his father that he would have to kill his son because he is Evil. Little Michael looked at the strange man and he told him to continue to look, then he saw his mother having a discussion about who was going to kill him. Then he saw his parents smiling and laughing saying to each other that it would be a blessing to kill that Devil. Little Michael looked at the strange man with tears in his eye's and told him that he would be ready for them. The strange man told him to except Satan as his lord and master then he will grant you the power to destroy your enemies, then he told him to kneel down. Little Michael kneeled down in front of the strange man and yelled out he denounced God and accepted Satan as his lord and saver and as soon as he done that his heart stopped. The strange man stood over his body and uttered some words" Oh Evil father from below! Fill this boy with your

Wicket soul! And Little Michael body began to glow and shake. At the Church Mitchell was on his knees asking God for the straight to deal with what was about to happen, Then an angel appeared in back of him and told him that his son was tricked into accepting Satan as his Lord and saver. Mitchell turned and looked at the angel with anger in his eyes, then he said to the angel why did God allow this and the angel told him that greater people has been tested by the lord! Then the Angel told him that people God chose to deliver his word all had their loyalty tested. Mitchell looked up at the angel with tears in his eyes and told him that is his only son and he don't know if he could do it. The angel waved his hand across his face and he began to see all of the Evil that his child done to the people in the Neighborhood. Then he began to see the entire young people killed in the school. Mitchell dried his eyes and asked the angel was there any way to save his son soul! The Angel looked at him and told him that if he comes back to God before it is too late. Mitchell bowed down and thanked the Angel, he then got up and walked towards the front door when the angel spoke out and said that Little Michael loves being evil. Mitchell looked at the angel and told him that he would try to reach him. Then he walked out the door and went home and told Ebony that there was still away they could save their child, Ebony looked at Mitchell and told him that if they could do it she was all for it but if not he must be destroyed. Mitchell looked at his wife with a sad look and told her that he knows, and then he went into the bedroom. Ebony began cooking dinner and Mitchell took a shower, after dinner they sat at the table with tears in their eyes wondering were did everything go wrong. On the other side of town Little Michael and the strange man were walking threw Bryan park when they saw two men sitting on the bench shooting heroin. The strange man looked at Little Michael and told him that the two men were a waste to this world, plus a disgrace to God himself. Then he told him that people like that end up in Hell anyway so why not send then there now! Little Michael looked at the strange man and turned to the two men and began staring at them mumbling strange words" blaze and burn you fool of death! Its time to fry until nothings left! Then his eyes turned red like fire and the two men pulled out of their pockets a stem and a vial of crack, then they put it to their mouth to smoke it when it exploded in their face. The explosion was so powerful that the two caught on fire and burned to ashes, the screams were so intense that the ground shook. The strange man began to laugh and patted Little Michael on the top of his head and said you are truly Lucifer's child. Then they both stared at the ground and it busted open with flames bursting out, the two jumped into the flames and disappeared. That evening during Servest Mitchell were preaching to the congregation about the signs of the last days and why God chooses his warriors. The whole Church eyes were glued on Mitchell as he broke it down about how the lord protects his children from the evilness of Satan. The people in the church began giving praise to the Lord and his message, out side of the Church stood and a young man smoking a joint. After Mitchell finished speaking the young man walked up to the church with his eyes glowing, he then opened the door and walked in and stood in the al. Mitchell looked at the young man and then began calling out for God to remove the Demon from that young man body, the young man looked at Mitchell and began screaming. Mitchell stepped off of the pull pit and walk towards the young man and his voice rang out in a demonic tone "Stay back Mother Sucker! Get your Holy crap out of my freaking face! But Mitchell continued to towards the young man shouting "Devil be gone from this innocent soul of God! The young boy began shaking and screaming then he fell to the floor and turned into a strange looking wolf creature. Mitchell pulled out a bottle of Holy water and pored it into his hands, the beast then leaped at Mitchell and he slammed his hands on the face of the beast and said a prayer, then the creatures face began to burn. The beast let out a horrifying yell as it fell to the floor the wolf like beast separated from the young man and burned to ashes and disappeared. The Church stood there in shock because it happens so fast and the Minister showed his members that God was in the house. Mitchell began felling stronger in faith and he then realized that God had chosen him for the battle. After Servest Mitchell and Ebony were walking home when a ball of fire appeared and Little Michael and the strange man walked out. Mitchell and ebony stood there in shock as they gaze upon their son looking evil as ever. Little Michael walked up to his father and asked him did he miss him; then he looked at mother and told her that he knows their plan but they will fail. Mitchell stood in front of his wife and told Little Michael that he was sorry that his lack of faith did that to him. Little Michael looked at his father and told him that he was grateful that his faith wasn't a joke, then he looked at his mother and told her that he know she didn't want him any way. Ebony looked at Little Michael and told him that he was wrong, she always loved him and always will but his soul is Evil. Little Michael looked at his mother and told her that if he is evil it's because they allowed it to happen to him. Mitchell looked at him with tears in his eyes and told him that he was right but he is very sorry about that, he then told him that because of there lack of faith it happen. The strange man looked at Mitchell and told him that he could give his soul for his son soul! Mitchell looked at the strange man and told him that he will win back his son soul and he will destroy him. The strange man looked at Mitchell with anger in his eyes and told him that he can destroy his whole community if he wanted too! Mitchell stood in front of his wife and told the strange man as long as God is in my life I will fear no evil. The strange man backed off and uttered that this was not his fight, he then looked at Little Michael and they walked away. Ebony tried to call Little Michael back but Mitchell told to let him go! She looked at him with great disappointment in her eyes. Mitchell looked at his wife and told her that that's not their son, it's a demon and this is the beginning of the battle the Angels talked about! Then he hugged her and told her that this is the time to be strong and not show weakness. Ebony wiped the tears from her eyes and looked at her Husband and told him that he was right, and then they held hands and went home. As they walked up to there building two teenagers were standing in front smoking, Mitchell and his wife walked up to the building and the two teens stepped in front of them. Mitchell looked at the two and asked to please let them pass and they asked why they should!

Mitchell slowly let go of his wife hand and told the teens that he know who they are and they don't scare him. The two teens looked into his eyes and walked away laughing, Mitchell grabbed his wife hand and they went up stairs. On the other side of town Little Michael and the strange man were in front of a junior high school in Patterson New Jersey, the strange man looked at Little Michael and asked him how should he destroy them? Little Michael looked at the strange man and asked him what did they do! And the strange man looked at Little Michael and told him that they all have sex with animals. Little Michael looked at him funny, and then he asked him was he for real then the strange man turned to him and told him not to question him. Little Michael looked at the strange man and asked him who was he talking to like that and the stranger looked shocked, he then looked at Little Michael and told him that he was playing with fire boy then Little Michael looked at him and said your right. Then he rose up his hand and two large balls of fire came from out of nowhere and hit the strange man and exploded. When the fire died down the strange man was gone and there were no traces of him anywhere. Little Michael looked around to see if he saw him but he was nowhere to be found, he then began to walk away when two fiery hands came up and grabbed him by the ankles and pulled him under. A few minutes later the ground opened up and Little Michael and The strange man jumped out in flamed and then they turned back to normal. They stared each other down for a moment then they walked to the Connor and sat on the bench, Little Michael looked at the strange man and told him that he don't want anything to happen to his parents and the strange man told him that he will die by his fathers hands. Little Michael looked at the strange man and told him that he is the only one allow to touch him, no one else! Then Little Michael stood up and asked the strange man who was next on the chopping block. The Strange man stood up and raised his cane and a large ball of fire appeared and they walked threw it, they ended up in front of an old Motel on 42nd street, the place was full pimps, hookers and tricks. The strange man looked at looked at Little Michael and he told the strange man that a pack of beast should go in and feed on their dirty flesh; the strange man looked at him and said time to become a man. He then rose up his hand and waved it across the front wall, the wall turned into a door and them both walked threw it. On the other side stood eighteen beautiful naked women, Little Michael looked at the strange man and he told Little Michael its time to show what you're made of. He then clapped his hand and Little Michael was in bed with the women having sex for his first time. On the other side of town Mitchell and Ebony were in bed sleeping when out side of the Building a group of young boys were gathering in front. The young boys began going into the building and up the stairs to the Robinsons apartment, the mission was to kill them before midnight, to prevent him from destroying their new master. Then an angel appeared in front of the Robinson's bed and woke them up. The angel told them that Satan has sent his Demon to kill them and they needed to get up, the two got up and the angel waved his hand over them in a circler motion. A shell of protection covered them and other angel began to appear with swards drawn. Out side of the Robinsons door, the demon began turning into creatures then busted into the apartment and was met by Gods angels. The battle began as Gods angels began to slay all the demons one by one and as their body parts fell so did the strange man; He began feeling weak and drained out so left Little Michael alone and went to see what was happening at the Robinson. He reappeared on the floor of the Robinsons and saw two of Gods angels walking out with them and when they went down stairs he looked into the apartment and saw his Demons chopped in pieces. Weakness hit him so hard that he fell to the floor and crawled over to the body parts of his Demons and began picking it up and placing it back into his chest. As the body parts dissolved back into his chest he began to grow stronger, after gaining his strength back he disappeared. He then reappeared in the room where Little Michael having sex, he sat back in the chair and continued to watch Little Michael un-virgin ceremony, the Strange man sat there thinking about what he just seen, the Robinson were protected by God. He began rocking back and forth in his chair thinking of ways to deceive the Robinsons into dropping their guards, finally Little Michael finished with the hookers. He then got up and walked over to the strange man looking evil as ever, Little Michael stood in front of the strange man naked with his eyes glowing. "What's up my Botha? Little Michael uttered! I feel freaking great! I rocked the mess out of those chicks's man, if this is what hell is like; I am down! The strange man smiled and told him to get dressed because he doesn't want to be looking at his private. Little Michael looked at himself and said oh shoot! He then walked away and put on his clothes, and then he came back ready to kill. The strange man stood up and told Michael to follow him and they went back to the junior high school, Little Michael looked at the strange man and said you don't have to say a word! Little Michael's eyes began to glow and pack of dog like creatures appeared and ran into the school and killed them all. As the creatures were tarring them apart Little

Michael grew stronger and stronger. The strange man looked at him smiling then waved his hand and the ground busted open and they both jumped into it and it closed up. At the Church, Mitchell and his wife were sitting trying to understand what had just happen in their apartment; one of the angels told them that their child had been chosen. Mitchell looked at the angel and asked him what was he talking about and the angel told him that Little Michael was not of him. Ebony looked at the angel and told him that he was mistaking and the angel told her that she was taking by an unclean spirit, and then he told her that's why she was in so much pain. Ebony began to cry and Mitchell hugged her telling her that it will be alright! The angel told them that in order to have a normal life they must destroy what their sins has created, The Robinson dried their eyes and then asked the angel how could they destroy something so evil? The angel told Mitchell that he would not be alone in the fight! Mitchell looked at the angel and asked him what do he have to do? The angel pulled out a dagger from his bag and told him when the blade glows plunge it into his heart and twist. The angel then told him that if he kills the Demon inside of his son, he would be blessed with another one. Mitchell looked at his wife and told her that their son must be stopped, and that many innocent people may be killed if they don't and Ebony agreed. The Robinson family has been choosing by the dark forces to bring forth a child of Evil and have their faith tested at the same time. Ebony had decided to do her part in putting an end to Little Michael's rain of horror also they had made up their minds about starting over again. The hours began to past and the time drew near when the final battle was about to take place. Mitchell looked at his wife and told her that if he didn't survive the battle, he wanted her leave and re-marry. Ebony looked at him and told him to stop talking negative and keep the faith. Then she hugged him and told him that God protects his people and never lets them down and Mitchell smiled and walked out the door. As he walked down the hallway he began stronger in faith and much stronger in strength. Mitchell walked down the stairs and went out the building to the courtyard and saw Little Michael standing there with the strange man and his friends. Mitchell stopped in his tracks and Little Michael looked at him then began walking towards him, Mitchell yelled out "stop son! Michael stopped and yelled out "oh faithful father! Can you really kill your own child? Mitchell pulled out his Bible then told Michael if he did not repent for his sins, he will strike him down. Little Michael smiled and began walking towards him and so did the strange man and his friends. Mitchell backed up a bit then stopped tracks; an army of angels stood behind him ready for battle, Mitchell turned around and was surprised. God had sent an army of Angels to help Mitchell in his fight; Mitchell looked up and gave thanks. Little Michael seen what just happen and turned looking for the strange man and he was no where to be found, Little Michael and turned back and yelled out" Where are you! You are blinking Wimp! But the strange had abandoned him in his time of need. Little Michael became furious then looked at his father and said" its time old man! Then he leaped at him and Mitchell drew back his arm and punched Little Michael in his face, knocking him on the ground. Mitchell seen that Michael could be hurt so he tried to reason with him but he didn't want to hear anything. Little Michael got up and attacked his father again, blow for blow the battle continued, the Demons that were with Little Michael attacked the father and the Angel intervened. The Angels pulled out their swards and began cutting down the demons by the dozens, in the mean time Mitchell started to get tried and his son began getting the best of him and Mitchell grew weak. Little Michael stood over him laughing" what's up old man? You really though you could take on me? I am the next prince of Darkness! Raising his arms in the air! Mitchell then kicked him in the stomach lifting him into the air. Little

Michael landed in a pile of garbage nearby; Mitchell got up and looked around and saw the Angels in battle with Little Michael's friends. In the Church, Ebony was preaching, asked God to protect her husband in battle and the Church door flung open. There stood Church members from all over the neighborhood ready to go to battle; Ebony stepped off of the pulpit and lead then to the battle. They matched to the courtyard and saw Mitchell and Gods Angel in battle with Little Michael and his followers so they rushed in. The elderly, the young, the middle age all joined into the battle, all had tremendous amounts of strength. Bodies were being tossed around like rag dolls, Good was over coming Evil and Little Michael followers were losing the battle. He saw his followers dropping like flies and fear began to set into Little Michael heart, he began to realize that this was for real and his father was truly going to kill him. Little Michael looked at his father as he drew near, so he turned to look for the strange man but he was know were to be found. Michael became upset and turned in a large wild beast and began attacking the angel ripping them to pieces and eating their body parts. All hell had broke lose in the court yard as bodies of demons, angels and humans fell to the ground. Little Michael began to grow in size and his hands became shape as razors, he then began to slice chunks of flesh from the body of the angels and people. Ebony and the other Church members began getting scared and began backing off when they saw what he had become. Little Michael sensed the fear in the Church members he attacked them then he began ripping and tearing them to pieces. Little Michael leaped at his mother and Mitchell pulled her away in time, Mitchell then stood in front of his wife and shouted that it was he that he wanted and not her. Little Michael stopped and turned towards Mitchell and began to growl, showing all of his razor shape teeth as he slowly crept up on him. Mitchell slowly backed up and pulled the Blade from his pocket and when Little Michael leapt at them Mitchell went to plunge it in him when the strange man appeared and snatched him into hell. The ground closed up and Mitchell fell to the ground feeling weak, the angel gathered around him helping him up. They then helped him to the bleaches and told him that the war was not over and to be ready at all times. Then the angels disappeared and the Robinson went back upstairs badly engorged from the battle, Ebony began crying about the church members that were killed in battle. Mitchell hugged his wife and told her that they were brave soldiers for the Lord and they are in Heaven, then he kissed her and told her that they fought for good. He then began kissing his wife and cur resting her, telling her that he loves her with all of his heart. The two then went to bed then fell asleep, around 1:40 in the morning the Robinsons herd a strange rapping on their front door, they then heard a whispering voice saying" Open the fuing door! Suckers! Mitchell slowly got out of the bed and slowly walked towards the door with the blade drawn and you heard the voice on the other side say" Oh God! He still has the blade! And the voice stopped! Mitchell snatched open the door with the blade in his hand by the hall was pitched black and no one was in site. Mitchell slams the door and rested his body against it huffing and puffing in fear, and then he looked to the Heavens and asks God for the strength to bare the madness. Then he walked back to his bed room and found the strange man holding a strange looking blade to his wife Ebony's neck. Mitchell stood there in fear, the strange man then told him to hand over the blade before he personally drags her to hell. Mitchell pulled out the knife and handed it to him when the blade began to glow and it disappeared. The strange man began screaming then he sliced his wife throat and threw her to the floor, Mitchell ran over to her screaming for God to help him and two angels appeared and the strange man disappeared. As the blood spilled on the floor, Mitchell screamed with tears running down his face and the angels appeared over Ebony's bleeding body and one of the angels bended over her and placed his hand on her and began to heel. Mitchell fell back and stared at the angel and clashed his hands together, thanking God for sending the angels to him. He then ran over to his wife and hugged her and asked her was she alright, she looked at him and whispered in a low voice that she was ok and God was by her side. On the other side of town on the west side of Fourth Street in a gay bar, a man and his boyfriend were having an argument about cheating and the strange man stepped out of the darkness. He then walked up to the two and asked was there anything he can do to help and one of the gay men looked at him and screamed" you!! You're that mother sucker that gave my man forty stitches in his back side! The strange man looked at the guy's boyfriend and said "what's up Willie! I think you should have told him about us! Then he turned to the other one and said "did he tell him about the time the sperm from his private got stuck in his throat. Then he looked at both of them and burst into flames and burned them into ashes, and then he went into the bar and began killing everyone in the place. A few minutes later he came out of the bar laughing and rubbing his private saying" God blessed you for making gays! Then out of the darkness Little Michael came with four of his friends; what's up Brother! The word is that you cut my mothers throat! He looked at the strange man with fire in his eyes, and then Little Michael began screaming that he told him not to touch them. Then strange man looked at Little Michael and told him that he better back off before he bust him up and then pop him, Little Michael looked at him and told him with rage in his eyes that he was about to beat him to death. The strange man looked at Little Michael and then began to grow into a huge colossal type of creature and Little Michael changed into a large beast like creature with razor shape claws. The two leaped into battle ripping and tearing into each others bodies, and then they began wrecking and destroying everything that was in their path. Thrustful jabs and thunderous blow echoed threw the air as the two battled, the strange man began getting the best of Little Michael and his friends seen that Little Michael started falling in battle so they all turned into the same type of beast and attack the strange man. The battle began to even out, then Little Michael and his friends went in for the kill and they all jumped on him, and tour the strange man to pieces then his body began to burn and descends back to hell. Little Michael and his friends began to turn back into their human form, and then they began walking the streets looking for more people to join their army or be destroyed by his hands. Little Michael began to feel like he was a god and no one would be able to touch him and his evil began to fully take over. Little Michael and his friends walked to a nearby bench and sat down, then he bent over, resting his elbows on knees (with his hands placed under his chin) then he turned and looked at his follower and told them that was sick of bull crapping around and that he wanted become the true ruler of the Heavens and the Earth. Then he got up and looked at the others and told them that the time as come for the real ruler to come forth and they all stood up and raised their arms. Then a ball of fire appeared and they all walked into the flames and disappeared and the streets turned back to normal, that morning people where on the streets looking around for Little Michael and his gang but they where no where to be found. Weeks began to past and the people began letting down their guards and went back to their normal lives. Mitchell and Ebony grew older and their faith grew stronger, Ebony kept having nightmares about the battle between the Church and her son Demonic army. The neighborhood began to get brighter and the children in the area began to come back out and return to their old routines. The police patrolling the areas also the Churches in the Neighborhood began giving functions in Mitchells honor for his fearless battle with Evil, the people voted him as the city mayor and the Robinsons began to move up in life. Mitchell began to use his power to clean up his area and open up more jobs also programs for the youth. Ebony later had two other children (Kevin and Alice) by Mitchell and they raised them in the Church. Ebony later became a school teacher and Mitchell moves them to their own home in the Pocono Mountains. Years began to past and the children grew older and so did Mitchell and Ebony, Kevin at the age of eleven began seeing strange faces staring at him when he was going to school and his sister Alice who was nine began hearing someone calling her name from the darkness. Kevin became very active in Church and his sister was also, their faith was strong and their connection with God was unbelievable, Kevin often found him self seeing things that no one else could see and his sister Alice found herself bring peace to the most negative people. By the time Kevin and Alice reached their late teens, Mitchell and Ebony was at their retirement age. Kevin became a junior Deacon and Alice Deaconess. Mitchell and Ebony raised their new children without a mention of their older brother Michael, but for some reason Alice felted that her parent were holding back a secret. Every time they would sit down to dinner Alice would look at her Mother and ask her why was she hearing voices saying that he was her brother. Kevin just looked his parents and shook his head , then when he seen that her question was getting their Mother and Father upset he would asked Alice to just forget it and she would stop. Alice then got up from the table and asks to be excused then she would go into her bed room and read the Bible. Mitchell then looked at Ebony and told her that one day they would have to tell them the truth about Michael and Ebony cried. Mitchell then would get up and go over and hug and kiss her. Kevin looked at his parents and asked them who was Michael and why was mom crying? Mitchell looked at his son and told him that Michael was his Evil older brother; Kevin just looked at him as he began telling him about Little Michael and the strange things that happen to him and his wife. The first thing he told him how he and his wife had been punished by God for turning their backs on him and how God allowed the Devil to test their faith. He then sat down and began telling Kevin about the strange dreams and how they were visited by spirits about their son being Evil and one day one of them would have to destroy him. In the Room Alice heard her father talking to her older brother so he she put down the bible and slowly walked to hear what they were talking about. Kevin looked in shock as his father told him about the strange way that Little Michael was behaving and how people were found dead in their area and no one knew how it happen, then he told Kevin that Michael began hanging a strange man. Then he told him about the day when he had to make the decision to either kill his son or let him kill all man kind. Kevin's eyes began to water as his father continued to tell him about the crazy thing that began to happen in Church and how god sent Angels to help him destroy Michael and his followers. Alice peeped out her head from the Connor then slowly crept into the Kitchen and sat on her mothers lap and hugged her. Mitchell then told Kevin that he knows that the fight is not over and that Michael may just kill him this time in battle. Kevin looked at his father and said that he would never let that happen; Alice looked at her father and said that she wouldn't let that happen either. Mitchell stood up and told then that Little Michael was heartless and that he was too old to fight him and Kevin stood up and told his father that he wasn't and he would protect him. Ebony looked at her children and told them that God would not let anything happen to their father so stop talking like that. Mitchell looked at Ebony and told her that the Lord had gave then warriors ready for battle, then he walked over to Kevin and told him that the Devil tricked his brother but he wont trick him. Kevin smiled and then hugged his father; Alice stood up and told her father that God told her that he would guide them to victory again. Ebony looked at her husband and told him that she was very proud of them also she can feel the presence of the Lord in them. Alice and Kevin went to hug their mother and gave her a kiss also, and then they looked at their father and told him that they feel confident that they will destroy him. They all gave each other a group hug and they went to into their rooms, Mitchell and Ebony went to their room and lay down until they fell asleep. Around 4:00 a.m. in their old neighborhood, a crowd was gathering out side of their old building, an elderly lady was walking past the building when a large dresser fell down from the roof and crushed her into a spot of blood. The police and the people in the neighborhood all gathered to see what had happen, Little Michael and his followers stood in the shadows smiling. Little Michael and his friends turned into wolves and attacked the people that was standing out there, they brutally killed everyone there. After killing all the people out their Little Michael looked up to his parents window and decided to pay them a visit, he then called his followers and they went to pay his parents a visit but when the y broke into the apartment, there found it empty. Little Michael looked around with anger glairing in his eyes, he looked around and punched a large hole in the wall and then screamed" where the heck are they? When did they leave? Then they all turned into dogs and left the apartment, the police stood out side the building waiting for the coroner to come when

Little Michael and his followers broke threw the doors and attacked them. By the morning came the streets where filled with dead bodies badly ripped to pieces, When the other police showed up and saw the body parts of their follow officers, they became sick. The neighborhood went into an up raw and the people started becoming frightened all over again. The skies began to darken and the area started falling apart, the police went into full panic alert as they reached out for help from the army. Months and years began to past and things got worst, the dead toe amount rose higher then ever and people in the neighborhood found themselves moving out as fast as they could. Around 8:40 p.m. Little Michael and his people showed up at his father's old church and busted in the doors and found the Church full over Hispanic people, Little Michael looked shocked. The people in the church looked at him as he walked in asking where Mitchell Robinson was, the people looked at him like he was crazy. The Minister of the church asked who was Mitchell Robinson and Little Michael screamed "the Freaking Minister of this Church! Then he looked at his followers and told them to kill every one in the Church and the Minister walked off the pull pit and lifted up his arms and a light appeared and blew Little Michael and his friends out of the front door, then a army of Angel came walking out in full battle gear. Little Michael and his Followers got off of the ground then walked away, Michael looked back and shouted that it was not over yet! Then a large ball of fire appeared and they walked into it, then it disappeared. The angels looked at each other and one by one they all began to fade away and the people in the church began to awaken from a deep sleep. That evening when the Robinsons were at church service, an Angel appeared in the back of the church, Ebony recognized him while she was preaching and stopped. The Angel just looked at her and Ebony fell into an hypnotic state then began speaking in the angels voice warning them that Little Michael was on his way to them. Mitchell stood up and told the Church that Evil has found them and it is time for them to trust in God and his glory. The church stood up and began to pray for victory as the choir song" victory is mine! The spirit of the Lord was in the place and the church began to rock for the Lord. Bishop Robinson began preached like he never did before and the Children of the Lord were filled with the spirit, as the musicians played and the choir song, the doors flung open. There stood Little Michael and his followers; Mitchell looked at Little Michael with a serious look on his face. Michael looked at his father and yelled out" Hey Pop! Your Demon son is home! Mitchell looked at Little Michael and asked him was he ready to be saved then he asked to come in and when he tried he began to burn. Little Michael jumped back and yelled out that they had to come out of their one day, Mitchell told Little Michael that he was not afraid and be his ready for battle. Then he took off his robe and stepped off of the pull pit and walked toward the front door, all the people in the Church stood up and followed him. His wife and children walked behind him into battle, when they stepped out of the Church the streets were filled with Demons. The church member began singing Victory is mind! Then the sky opened up and Gods Angels appeared everywhere, soon Little Michael were out numbered and the head angel told Mitchell he would know when its time to strike and the angel went into battle. The mountains became a battle zone in front of the Church, the followers of Little Michael began to fall all around him, Little Michael pulled out a dagger and threw it at his father and Mitchell caught it. Mitchell looked at the head angel and he gave him the sign and Mitchell attacked, blow for blow father and son afflicted on each other. Little Michael began remembering when they asked him to leave and how he defended them against the strange man, and then he broke into rage. Little Michael drawled up some enormous amount of strength and punched his back into the Church and threw the podium. Ebony seen that and screamed and his children ran into the Church to attend to their father, Ebony ran toward Little Michael and he slapped her to the ground. The battle continued and Little Michael began yelling for his father to continue the fight but Mitchell was unconscious. A few minutes later Kevin came walking out of the Church yelling you hurt my father! Little Michael looked at him laughing, "So the old man is hurt! Kevin stood tall and looked at Little Michael and told him that he is ready to fight his father's battles now. Little Michael looked at Kevin and said "Ok little brother! Then Michael threw a punch at Kevin but he was to fast for him. Little Michael kept trying to hit him but he kept missing, the Lord blessed Kevin with the power to see what was going to happen before it happens; " stand still you little Freak! Michael yelled out in rage! Kevin continued to see all the moves Little Michael was about to make and he had a counter attack for it. A light covered Kevin and he began going blow for blow with his older brother, in this battle Little Kevin began getting the best of Michael and the battle became fierce. Kevin seen Michael growing tired so he picked up his speed and began to tire him out, Ebony came out and seen Kevin battling with Michael and Alice looked at Michael then told her mother that it wasn't too late for Michael to be saved and Ebony looked in amazement. The battle between Kevin and Michael went on for hours until Little Michael began to grow tired, Mitchell woke up and slowly walked to the front door of the Church. He saw Kevin in battle with his Michael and also he was getting tired so he pulled out the dagger that the Angel had gave him and threw it to Kevin. Kevin caught the dagger and rammed it into Little Michaels heart, Little Michael broke into a rage and tried to grab Kevin but still he was too quick. The blade began to glow and Little Michaels eyes rolled up in his head and he fell to the ground, Alice ran over to him and touched his hand and a bright light filled his body then he died. Alice then said a prayer for Little Michaels soul and two spirits emerged from the body, One Evil and one Good, she then raised her hand in victory and the Evil spirit exploded while the good spirit floated off to the Heavens. Alice stood up and looked at her father and told him that the Evilness in back where it belongs, then Mitchell and Ebony slowly walked over to Michael's body and saw the Child they once loved lying there. Kevin looked up and saw the skies clearing up the Blackness began to brighten up, Kevin then fell down exhausted from the battle. Mitchell picked up his son and hugged him, then they called out to the lord and waited for the police in front of the Church, The police and EMS came and the Robinsons explained what happen. The officer where about to arrest Little

Kevin when an Angel appeared and touched the officer's hearts, the offices took the handcuffs off of Kevin and told his parents to take him home! The Robinsons gave each other an hug and went into the church to pray, Mouths and years began to pass and the streets where once again safe, the flowers once again began bloom and happiness sprouted out from the darkness. Mitchell and Ebony grew older and their Children became ministers in the Church, Kevin was now twenty one and Alice was eighteen years old, both graduated from school with honors. Alice later began to teach Bible studies and Kevin ended up becoming a fiery Minister like his father, Gods glorious light has once again shined upon the land and the Robinsons rain victorious over Evil. Sunday morning; around 10:45 a old man came walking into the church asking for some one to pray for his soul, one of the deacons helped the elderly man to the front. Mitchell was sitting in the Bishops chair and Ebony was sitting in the First ladies chair, the place was full of the Holy Spirit and all was joist to the Lord. Alice stood up and looked at the elderly looking man and recognized who it was, the Deacons held him up as he whispered in a low pitch voice asking Kevin to asked God for forgiveness. Alice then walked up to the elderly man and told him that God had already forgiven him that why he is still alive now. The elderly man looked at Alice then told her thank you and Alice smiled and said your welcome big brother! Mitchell and Ebony looked in total shock as they got out of their seats and rushed over to Michael and hugged him crying. Kevin looked at the elderly man as he slowly walked off the podium and towards him, "brother! Brother! Kevin utter! Then an angel appeared and told them that the Lord has destroyed the evilness in him and Alice was the reason he was forgiven. Michael began crying telling his parents that he was sorry and wanted to be apart of the family again, Mitchell hugged his son crying telling him that he forgive him and love him dearly. The Angel walked over to Little Michael and touched his heart and the gray and rankles disappeared, he then began to stand up strait and Michael looked at his mother and told her that he loves her. Little Michael horror was no more and the Robinson family had survived the hell that rained upon them, Michael Robinson gave his life to God and slowly began to forget the horrors that he went threw as a child.

CPSIA information can be obtained
at www.ICGtesting.com
Printed in the USA
LVOW01s1944211016

509645LV00006B/19/P